THE DIFFERENCE
OF ARI STEIN

THE DIFFERENCE
OF ARI STEIN

by Charlotte Herman

Pictures by Ben Shecter

Harper & Row, Publishers
New York, Hagerstown, San Francisco, London

THE DIFFERENCE OF ARI STEIN

THE DIFFERENCE OF ARI STEIN
Text copyright © 1976 by Charlotte Herman
Illustrations copyright © 1976 by Ben Shecter
All rights reserved. No part of this book may be used or reproduced in any manner whatsoever without written permission except in the case of brief quotations embodied in critical articles and reviews. Printed in the United States of America. For information address Harper & Row, Publishers, Inc., 10 East 53rd Street, New York, N.Y. 10022. Published simultaneously in Canada by Fitzhenry & Whiteside Limited, Toronto.
Library of Congress Catalog Card Number: 75-25406
Trade ISBN 0-06-022309-X
Harpercrest ISBN 0-06-022310-3
FIRST EDITION

If I am not for myself, who will be for me?
And if I am only for myself, what am I?
And if not now, when?

—HILLEL

For Mel, who's really Moshe
with love and thanks
for taking me there

1

Sometimes you have to make a choice. And sometimes the most unlikely person helps you make it. Take me and Maxie Friedman. My mother says I was on the verge of becoming a bum because of him. Little does she realize that Maxie was the one who helped me make my choice. Though he didn't know it at the time.

I first met Maxie on a hot June Monday about a year ago, in front of 2–4 Nass Walk in Brooklyn, where I had moved from Rivington Street on the Lower East Side. I remember because it was June 1944, just after D-Day, when General Eisenhower and the American troops invaded France.

Maxie was standing on a ladder, blacking out the N in NASS on the street sign. I was sitting on the johnny pump, laughing and hoping he wouldn't get caught. "Does it look all right from down there?" he called.

"You can't see the N anymore, if that's what you mean," I shouted back.

Maxie scurried down the ladder. When he reached the ground, he stood back to admire his handiwork.

"Perfect!" he said. And he pulled out a handkerchief and mopped the sweat from his face.

"Aren't you worried about getting into trouble?" I asked. "Violating city property?"

"Heck no. I'm too young to go to jail. So what could happen? Besides, if I don't do it first, some kid'll beat me to it."

Maxie dragged the ladder over to the apartment building and left it against the brick wall. I gave him a quick once-over. He was a big guy with dark eyes and black hair, sort of curly. I could see his muscles bulging underneath his T-shirt.

"Are you the kid who just moved into the Cohens' apartment?" he asked.

"I don't know the name of the people, but it's the one on the third floor near the fire escape."

"Yeah, that's it. You've got the best apartment in the building. Right near the roof. What's your name anyway?"

"Ari. Ari Stein."

His eyes rested on the skull cap I was wearing. "You sure don't look Jewish. If it wasn't for your beanie, I'd never know it."

"My beanie? Oh, you mean my *yarmulke*. Yeah, I guess it *is* a dead give-away."

"Now take me for instance," Maxie went on. "You can tell just by looking at me that I'm Jewish. Of course, I could pass for Italian too, but with a name like Maxie Friedman . . ."

2

"Yeah, that's a dead give-away too," I said.

My bottom felt sore from sitting on the pump, so I stood up and walked around. Standing next to Maxie, I could really appreciate the size of him. He was a good head taller than me. I guess he noticed the difference in our heights too.

"Hey, how old are you anyway?" he asked.

"Eleven."

"Oh, that's okay then," he said. "For a minute there, I thought you were a lot younger than that. You're not exactly what you'd call tall."

"I know. I suffer from a hereditary defect."

"No kidding? What's wrong with you?"

"I come from short parents."

"Okay," Maxie laughed. "I can take a hint. No more cracks about your size."

For a little while longer we admired the NASS WALK sign that didn't say NASS anymore, and I helped Maxie lug the ladder down to the basement so the super wouldn't yell at him. Then we walked up and down Nass Walk, and he showed me how some of the other kids had fixed up the signs. I had to admit that Maxie's was the most professional-looking one on the whole street.

When we got back to the building, I heard a voice calling, "Maxie, lunchtime! Go get Benjy. We're having salami." I looked up and saw some lady with her head sticking out of a second-floor window. I guessed it was Maxie's mother.

3

Maxie jabbed me in the arm. "Hey, how about you coming up and having lunch with me? It'll be nice eating with someone else besides Benjy. And maybe if you're with me, my ma won't all the time be telling me how I should eat all my food because there's a war on in Europe and children are starving."

"Won't your mother mind?" I asked. "She doesn't even know me."

"Heck no. She'll be glad to see me hanging around with somebody besides Brownie."

"Brownie? Is he a dog or something?"

"No, he's Isidore Brown. He lives across the street at 1–3. Everybody calls him Brownie."

"I like Isidore better," I said.

"Don't let him hear you say that," Maxie warned. "He'll really let you have it. Nobody, absolutely nobody, calls him Isidore. Not even his mother."

"About your salami," I said, as we started up the steps. "Is it kosher?"

"Kosher? Oh sure. My ma always buys her stuff at the deli on the corner. Kosher is all they sell there."

"That's good," I said. "Because kosher is all I eat."

"You really *are* Jewish, aren't you?"

"I try to be," I said.

We went up to my apartment so I could get permission to eat at Maxie's. Then we had to go get Maxie's brother, who was up on the roof with his pigeons. Maxie told me that Benjy was always with his pigeons, ever since he caught them a few weeks earlier.

4

It was almost impossible to find Benjy with all the clothes drying on the lines. We made our way through the sheets and towels. And ladies' underwear kept slapping us in the face. Maxie pointed to an enormous pair of ladies' bloomers.

"See that? That belongs to Fat Mrs. Silverman. All the big stuff here belongs to her. You can tell a lot about the people who live in the building just by looking at their laundry. Some of the ladies are sort of embarrassed, and they try to hide their underwear in between the sheets and towels. And others, like Mrs. Silverman, let them fly free for everybody to see. And another thing. Mrs. Silverman's husband doesn't wear pajamas. I've lived here for two years, and I've never once seen his pajamas on the line."

We finally found Benjy and his two pigeons behind some gray-white bath towels. His pigeon coop was made out of an old orange crate covered with chicken wire.

"Hey, Benjy, it's time for lunch," Maxie called.

"Okay, Maxie. I'm coming." Benjy looked up at me and smiled. He had a dirty face, and a front tooth was missing. He was a carbon copy of Maxie except for the muscles. I figured him to be about seven years old.

"Maxie, I want my pigeons to get babies. How do I get them to have babies?"

"Uh . . . it's lunchtime, Benjy. Let's go eat."

"Okay, Maxie. But how do I get my pigeons to have babies?"

"Uh . . . this here is Ari Stein. He's new in the building. He's going to eat with us. Aren't you, Ari?"

"Hi, Ari," Benjy said. "What about the babies, Maxie?"

Maxie looked to me for help. "You breed them, Benjy," I said.

"Yeah," Maxie put in. "You breed them."

Benjy grinned. "Is that all I have to do?"

"Yeah," Maxie said. "But you can breed them later. Let's go eat first."

Benjy kissed the pigeon he was cuddling and stuck it back into the coop with the other one.

The door to Maxie's apartment was open. We walked through the foyer and into the kitchen. Maxie's mother was standing at the sink with a pickle in her mouth. Three Shmulke Bernstein salamis hung next to the window in front of her. The whole kitchen smelled of pickles and salami. It reminded me of Rivington Street.

"Come in, come in," Mrs. Friedman said. "You must be Mrs. Stein's boy. Nice lady, your mother. I went upstairs before to say hello. But I didn't stay long. I'm not one to poke. . . ."

"Ma," Maxie interrupted, "can Ari eat lunch with us?"

"Of course, of course. Such a nice boy. Go wash and then we'll eat."

Maxie led the way to the bathroom, with Benjy following. Nobody had to show me the way, though.

Maxie's apartment was exactly like mine. Maxie and Benjy washed up first. Benjy didn't even bother to rinse the soap off. He just wiped the soapy dirt on the towel.

"Hey, dopey, look what you did to the towel," Maxie said. And he gave him a little shove into the sink. Then Benjy shoved Maxie into the sink. They took turns shoving each other into the sink, and I could see it was all in fun. I kind of wished I had a brother to shove into the sink.

"This is sure some fancy apartment," I said.

"Fancy? Are you kidding? It's a dump," Maxie said. "Just wait till the roaches start coming up from the basement. Every time the super forgets to call the exterminator, we have a roach war with the neighbors. The roaches crawl up from the basement to the ground floor. Then the people spray the place with Flit. That chases the roaches up to the first floor, where they get a second dose of the stuff. From the first floor they come to us. We get out this new stuff my pop brought home from the Brooklyn Navy Yard. DDT, one hundred per cent worth. And pow! Those roaches drop dead in the walls."

"Yeah, I heard of DDT. It's powerful, all right. But you can't use one hundred per cent worth. You'd drop dead too. It's more like five per cent, or maybe ten."

"So I exaggerated a little," Maxie said. He threw me the soap.

"It's still a nice place," I said. "My mother calls it a palace. We never had our own bathroom before."

8

Benjy looked at me like he wasn't hearing right. "No bathroom? What did you use?"

"Oh, we had a bathroom to use," I said. "But it was in the outside hallway. We had to share it with all the other people on the floor."

Maxie's mother was calling from the kitchen. "It takes so long to wash a few hands? Come. Lunch is ready."

Mrs. Friedman gave us hunks of salami stuck between fat slices of rye bread. We had pickles and Dr. Brown's soda. It was a rare treat for me to get a Dr. Brown's. My mother doesn't believe in soda. Not healthy, she says. Better to have orange juice. Between the pickles and salami, I thought I would need to chew a whole package of Sen-Sen. But everything tasted great.

Benjy only ate the middle of his sandwich and left the crusts. He left a piece of pickle too.

"Look at the food you're wasting, Benjy," Mrs. Friedman said. "It's a shame to waste food. Think of all the starving children in Europe."

Maxie looked at me and snickered.

"Mama," Benjy asked, "how does it help the starving children if I eat up all the food?"

"Never mind," his mother said. "Just eat."

"Hey Ari," Maxie said. "How about us going down to the boardwalk? There's something I want to show you." He whispered it so Benjy and his mother couldn't hear.

"Sure thing," I said. "I've never done that before.

I'll go tell my mother and meet you outside."

"Okay," Maxie said. "But don't take too long. We need lots of daylight."

"Can I go with you and Ari?" Benjy asked.

"Not today, kid," Maxie said. "You're not old enough."

I thanked Maxie's mother for the lunch. "Come any time," she said, smiling. "A nice boy like you is always welcome."

I walked out into the hallway. And from the moment I agreed to go to the boardwalk with Maxie, life for me was never quite the same.

2

We walked down West Fifth Street toward the beach. It was really something walking to the beach instead of having to ride there on a hot subway. Coney Island was practically next door to me. Not only was I living in a palace, I was living in a whole kingdom.

"How long did you say you've been living here?" I asked Maxie.

"Two years. Moved here from Brownsville when I was ten."

"That's a pretty tough place, Brownsville, isn't it?"

"Tough? Are you kidding? Why, that's the home of Murder, Inc. It's also the reason we moved. My ma said I was turning into a regular bum."

At the beach we climbed some steps and walked along the boardwalk that looked like it stretched for miles across the sand. It seemed to me that everyone in Brooklyn was out there on the boardwalk that afternoon—every kid, every mother with a baby carriage and every old lady who owned a beach hat and a shopping bag.

I looked across the water. It was calm and peaceful-

11

looking, and I found it hard to believe that at that very moment a war was taking place on the other side of the Atlantic.

Maxie came to a sudden stop. "Here's a good place," he said. "See where the boards are spread farther apart? We'll be able to see real good."

We climbed down the steps onto the sand and made our way under the dark, spooky boardwalk until we found the place that Maxie had pointed out.

"Okay," said Maxie. "This is how you do it." He tilted his head back. I tilted like he showed me, and then we peeked up through the crack, waiting for ladies to walk by so we could look under their dresses.

"There goes one," Maxie whispered.

"Where? Where?" I shouted. "Point it out. I can't see anything."

"Too late. You missed it. You've got to be fast. And keep your voice down. You don't want anyone to find us here, do you?"

I pushed my face up closer to the boards. Nothing.

Maxie poked me. "Quick! There's another one. Did you see that?"

"I can't see a thing. They're walking too fast."

"If we're lucky," Maxie said, "somebody will stop walking and stand still for a while. Then we can get a good look."

My neck was starting to ache from all that tilting. And sand was getting in my eyes. But nothing seemed to bother Maxie. He kept laughing and poking me.

"There goes one. And another. Wow! Did you see that? And that?"

"I don't see anything," I said. "Just a lot of feet."

"That's because you're not experienced. Wait till you've done this a few times. You'll get to know what to look for."

After we had been there for a while, I got to wondering if it was against the law to be hiding under the boardwalk, looking up ladies' dresses. Suddenly somebody tapped me on the shoulder. A husky voice said,

"Hey, what's going on around here?"

I spun around and came face to face with two guys. A tall, skinny one and a not-so-tall fat one. The skinny one was eating polly seeds, and the fat one was laughing.

"Scared ya, didn't I?"

"Oh, hi, Brownie," Maxie said to the fat one. "What are *you* doing here?"

"The same thing you're doing here," he said. "Move over and let me and Lippy get a look."

This kid Lippy spit out a shell. Then he and Brownie practically knocked us over as they pushed their way under the crack.

"Hey, quit shoving," Maxie said. "There's plenty room. And there are plenty other cracks in the boardwalk too, for that matter."

"Yeah," said Brownie. "But this one's the biggest, and you can see the most. Right, Lippy?"

"Right," said Lippy. And he spit out another shell.

13

Then the four of us crowded together under that one little crack and peeked up into that one little piece of daylight. Darn it! I still couldn't see anything.

The other guys seemed to be having a great time. Maxie and Brownie were laughing and poking. And Lippy was laughing and poking and spitting out shells. I felt stupid just standing there watching feet, so I did a little laughing and poking too. So what if I couldn't see anything? Who'd know the difference?

After a couple of minutes a lady walked overhead and stood still. I thought I caught a glimpse of something. Maybe it was my imagination. I'll never know. Because just then a voice boomed out.

"God will punish you!"

The four of us bumped heads as we jumped. An old lady in a black bathing suit was shaking her finger at us. "You should be ashamed. All of you. God will punish you for this."

"Oh, hello, Mrs. Plotkin," Maxie said. "We were just looking for some coins."

"With your face up in the air, you're looking for coins? Don't tell me you're looking for coins. I know what you're looking for, Maxie Friedman. And you should be ashamed."

She shook her finger at Brownie. "And shame on you too, Isidore."

Brownie glared at her. "My name's Brownie."

"Pardon me—Brownie. You should still be ashamed."

She shook her finger at Lippy. "I'm surprised at you, Leonard."

He spit out a shell. "Lippy."

"So let it be Lippy. You're a bad boy. It's not nice what you're doing."

Maxie edged toward me. "Millions of old ladies on the beach and we have to bump into one who lives right in our building."

Then the old lady started on me. "And you—whoever you are—you should also be ashamed."

I felt like she caught me without my clothes on. "I'm from the East Side," I said.

Maxie started to laugh. "Yeah. They don't have any boardwalks on the East Side, so he came to Brooklyn to look."

"That's enough from you, Maxie Friedman. Go home now."

"Aw, Mrs. Plotkin. Be a sport. We're just having a little fun."

"If you don't go home this minute, I'll tell your mother."

"Okay, okay. Relax. Don't get excited. We're going. But first, would you do us a little favor?"

"What kind of favor?" she asked.

"Would you go up on the boardwalk and stand over that crack for a while?" Then he burst out laughing and ran. And we all ran with him. Out from the shadows of the boardwalk, out into the sunlight and up the steps.

From down below we could hear, "Smart alec! You'll see. I'll tell your mother."

We raced up the boardwalk in the direction of

Coney Island. When we slowed down, Maxie introduced me to Brownie and Lippy as the new kid on Nass Walk. Maxie told me later that Lippy is really Lenny Lipshitz, but everybody calls him Lippy because he doesn't like his name, either.

As we walked, we passed stands of food, food and more food. And in front of all those stands, people were eating, eating and eating—franks and sauerkraut, corn on the cob with melted butter dripping all over, hot *knishes* and Italian ices. Boy, a person could live there forever with all that food! The smells were driving me crazy. I guess they were driving Brownie crazy too.

"Who's got money?" he asked. "I'm hungry."

"Are you kidding?" Maxie said. "When do we *ever* have money?"

Brownie snatched my *yarmulke* and began tossing it. "I thought maybe the new kid . . ."

"Ari," I said, grabbing my *yarmulke* out of the air. "And I don't have any money either."

"Don't people drink soda no more?" Brownie asked. "We checked the alleys for empties. Couldn't find nothin'. Could we, Lippy?"

Lippy spit out another shell. "Nothing," he said.

I was beginning to think this Lippy guy couldn't talk in sentences. He just kept on eating those polly seeds and spitting out the shells, leaving a trail on the boardwalk.

We started back toward West Fifth Street by way of

Surf Avenue. We passed the RKO Tilyou, where a Jennifer Jones movie was playing. Maxie said that if a Tarzan came around, we'd have to figure out a way to get some money so we could go see it.

"Speaking of movies," he said, "where's Buddy?"

"Uptown," Brownie said. "He thinks Monday's good for getting discovered."

"Wouldn't it be funny if he really got discovered?" Maxie asked. "We'd go to the movies and see a picture starring Buddy Rizzo, or we'd see him in a play on Broadway and run backstage to get his autograph."

"Buddy's dreamin'," Brownie said. "It can't happen."

"You never can tell. It might. He's a real handsome guy."

"He's pretty," Brownie said. "I wouldn't wanna be pretty. Would you, Lippy?"

"No," Lippy said.

"Neither of you guys have anything to worry about," Maxie said. "Anyway, if Buddy's around tomorrow, how about all of us going to Coney Island and treating Ari to an afternoon at Luna Park or Steeplechase? Sort of as a welcome to the neighborhood."

"But you don't have any money," I reminded him.

"Don't worry about it," he said. "You're our guest. Just leave everything to us. Right, guys?"

"Right," said Brownie.

"Right," said Lippy.

As we turned the corner of Nass Walk and West Fifth Street, Lippy picked up a penny he spotted lying in the gutter. A few minutes later we left him and Brownie in front of Murray's candy store, where Lippy stuck the penny in the polly-seed machine.

"So long, guys," Maxie said. "Don't forget about tomorrow."

I waved. "See ya."

"So long," said Brownie.

"So long," said Lippy. Two words. He was improving.

We trudged up the steps to our apartments. Maxie was lucky. He had one less flight to worry about.

"I sure am tired," I said when we got up to the second floor.

"Me too," Maxie said. "I'm beat. Maybe I'll see you later."

I barely managed that last flight. Too bad my palace didn't have an elevator. I was all set to knock on the door, when it opened, and somebody grabbed me.

3

"Lionel! Lionel darling!"

She was crushing me to death. "Aunt Marilyn," I gasped. "I can't breathe."

"Oh, I *am* sorry, darling. Here, let me look at you. My, you've grown."

"But you just saw me last week."

"It just goes to show you how time flies."

She drew me close and hugged me again. She felt like a pillow.

"I've come to give your mother some tips on fixing up your new apartment. But I must say, there's only so much one can do in a place like . . . oh well . . . Sarah, your Lionel is home."

"And your Lionel is tired from a hard day at the beach," I said as my mother came to the door. Her black hair was wrapped up in a dish towel.

"Then it's good you came home early, Ari. You can rest up before Pa comes home."

"Sarah, you're still calling him Ari? Even in the new neighborhood?"

"And why not? That's his name. It was my father's name, may he rest in peace. It's a fine name."

"Sarah, eleven years ago I thought you were wrong, and I still think you're wrong. He's an American boy. He should have an American name. What kind of American name is Ari?"

On and on she went, going over the same story I've heard a million times before. About how my parents gave me the Hebrew name *Ari*, and how my Aunt Marilyn, who used to be Malkeh before she decided to become modern, almost talked them into giving me an English name too. As she put it, "*Ari* means lion, so why not call him Lionel after that famous actor Lionel Barrymore."

Can you imagine that? Lionel Stein! It's crazy! Anyway, nobody in the whole world calls me Lionel except my Aunt Marilyn—who's really my Aunt Malkeh.

My mother went into the living room, followed by Aunt Marilyn, who kept after her, saying things like, "After all, Sarah, it *is* 1944."

"I know."

"This is America."

"Thank God. And in America a boy can have the name of Ari."

My mother started to rearrange the furniture. She put my father's favorite reading chair next to the window. Aunt Marilyn immediately dragged it across the floor and pushed it into a corner on the opposite side of the room.

"Sarah, darling, it does so much more for the room over here. Don't you think so, Lionel?"

"Abe likes to read by the window," my mother said. And she pushed the chair back to where she had it the first time.

"If he needs light, he can turn on a lamp," Aunt Marilyn said. She shoved it back into the corner.

"It's a waste of electricity to turn lights on in the daytime," my mother told her. And she pushed the chair over to the window, where it's been sitting ever since.

My mother fixed up the apartment just fine without Aunt Marilyn's help. The kitchen looked like we had been living in it for years. The familiar curtains were already hung up, and the charity boxes, the *pushkes* we call them, were on the window sill. The white Sabbath cloth was on the table instead of the everyday oilcloth.

"It's Monday, Ma. Why are you using the *Shabbos* tablecloth?"

"It's a special day for us, Ari. So it's only right that we use the special cloth. It's not every day a person moves into such a place."

My mother's face lit up as she looked around her kitchen. "Look, Malkeh. It's like a palace."

Aunt Marilyn shrugged. "Next to Rivington Street, anything would look like a palace."

My mother's smile began to fade. "It's a swell place, Ma," I said. "I wouldn't want to live anywhere else."

"Would you like to stay for supper, Malkeh?" my mother asked. "We have more than enough."

"I'd love to, but I really have to run. I'm meeting Michael in a half hour."

"How *is* Uncle *Moshe*?" I asked.

"Uncle *Michael* is just fine," she said abruptly. "Well, I really must be going. Good-bye, Lionel. Good-bye, Sarah."

"Good-bye, Aunt Marilyn."

"Good-bye, Malkeh."

She blew us a kiss and flew out the door. I ran to the window and waited until my modern Aunt Marilyn got into her modern '41 Mercury and sped away.

I had an hour left before supper, so I went to my room to relax. Some room. It was more like an overgrown closet. But it was all mine. And I even had my own bed. For eleven years my sleeping quarters consisted of a couch in the living room. Well, not the whole eleven years, of course. In the beginning I slept in a crib. But after that, I mean.

I brushed the sand out of my hair and plopped on the bed. I lay there thinking of Maxie and Brownie and Lippy and the polly seeds. Of Marilyn and Malkeh, Ari and Lionel, Moshe and Michael, old and modern, modern and old . . .

When my father came home, he kissed my mother and put his arm around me. A smile spread across his face. My father's a very handsome man, especially when he smiles. He has a severe case of premature grayness. When I was little, I used to think he was very old. Now I think he's very distinguished-looking.

"You fixed up the apartment very nice, Sarah," my father said. "And the *Shabbos* cloth . . . everything is beautiful."

My mother managed a faint smile.

My father looked at her. "Such a sad face on such a happy day?"

"Aunt Marilyn's been here," I said.

"Ah, I understand. Malkeh again. I'm afraid the years have shown us that my sister isn't the easiest person in the world to get along with."

"Maybe if you'd call her Marilyn," I suggested.

"I've tried," my mother said. "Many times I've tried to say Marilyn, but it keeps coming out Malkeh. She's not a Marilyn. But Malkeh isn't what bothers me. I was thinking of Etta. Abe, it's been five years since we've heard. Five years—and nothing."

My mother's face had that sad, faraway look I'd been seeing so often, whenever she spoke of her sister in Poland. I had an aunt and uncle in Poland. And three cousins; the youngest was a boy my age. My mother and her sister wrote to each other all the time and always sent pictures back and forth. But the last letter came when I was six—just about the time that Germany invaded Poland. She read that letter over and over, sometimes out loud but mostly to herself. She knew the words by heart. So did I: "Times are bad, Sarah. There are dark days ahead for the Jewish people."

"Come, come," my father said. "We can't let such thoughts spoil our first day here. Tell me, Ari, what did you do today?"

I told him about Maxie and how we went to the boardwalk. Of course I didn't say what we did there. I'm close to my father but not *that* close. And I told him about Brownie and Lippy and the polly seeds. "They're treating me to Coney Island tomorrow."

"I'm glad you were able to make such good friends so soon," my father said.

"They sound like nice boys," my mother added. She dropped some coins into the *pushkes*, and then we all sat down to supper.

Later that evening, when I went into the kitchen to say good night, I saw my mother sitting at the table with the letter in her hand. The faraway look was there. Poor Ma. I'll bet she was wondering if she'd ever hear from Etta and her family again. Or was that letter the last one? The very last. Maybe Hitler had already finished with them, and now there was nobody left.

4

I woke up to a trumpet blasting out something that sounded like "The White Cliffs of Dover." On Rivington Street I woke up to a violin a few times but never to a trumpet. Morty Gurdy used to play the violin. His mother was preparing him to become Jascha Heifetz.

My father had already left for his job in the mink shop. Before the war he drove a milk truck, and I used to go with him on his routes. Mostly I carried the unbreakables—the cheese and butter—but sometimes I even got to carry the empty bottles back to the truck.

Then the war came, and gas and tires were hard to come by. So he gave up the milk business and took this job in the mink shop. Now he sits at a sewing machine all day, sewing little minks together so some rich lady can have a mink coat.

He works hard to make enough money for us to live on. He even has to work on Sunday—in spite of the Blue Laws, which say that stores and businesses have to be closed on Sunday. But like all observant Jews, my father doesn't work on Saturday, our Sabbath. It would be hard to lose two days of pay each week, so he works on Sunday instead. Every so often he gets a ticket and has to pay a fine.

"Someday the laws will be changed," my father says, "so that Jews will be able to observe their Sabbath and still be able to work a six-day week."

My mother was in the hallway, talking to Mrs. Silverman. I could recognize her by the size of her rear.

"I didn't know Mrs. Silverman lived on our floor," I said to my mother when she came back into the apartment.

"How did you know that was Mrs. Silverman?" she asked.

"Uh . . . well . . . she just looks like a lady who'd be called Mrs. Silverman. Say Ma, listen to that trumpet. Can I take trumpet lessons? I think I'm musically inclined."

"I should say not. Violin, yes. But trumpet, no. You'll bust your lungs."

"I don't think I want the violin," I said. "I think two Jascha Heifetzes are enough." I sat down to my favorite summer breakfast of orange juice and Wheaties —"The Breakfast of Champions." I felt like Jack Armstrong, the All-American Boy I always listen to on the radio. Then I went out.

All the guys were in the gutter playing Johnny-on-a-pony. It was Brownie's turn to jump on top of Lippy. Well, poor Lippy practically got crushed under Brownie's tremendous weight. Brownie knocked the other guys over and sent them crashing to the pavement. They were just getting up and dusting themselves off when Maxie saw me. "Hey Ari. Come on over."

I walked over, and pretty soon I found myself standing in front of the most handsome guy I had ever seen. He was more than handsome. He was beautiful. He had black wavy hair, dark eyes and long lashes. He was tall and slim, and even an ordinary T-shirt and dungarees looked good on him. This kid *should* have been in the movies, he was so handsome. Handsomer than Gregory Peck, even. He reminded me of somebody, I couldn't think of who.

"Buddy, this here is Ari, the new kid I was telling you about. Buddy lives on the ground floor at 2–4," Maxie told me.

"Hi, Buddy," I said. "Did you have any luck yesterday?"

"Not a bit. I walked up and down Times Square and Forty-second Street a thousand times, and I hung around some of the theaters. But I didn't see anybody important and nobody important saw me. Once I saw a real tall guy walking in front of me. From the back he looked like Gary Cooper, but when I saw his front, he was somebody else." He talked very fast, like he had to catch the words before they ran away from him.

"Maybe all the movie stars and actors are taking their summer vacations in Hollywood," Maxie said.

"That's dumb," Brownie said. "Movie stars and people like that don't work. They don't need vacations. Right, Lippy?"

"Right. They just act in movies." I figured when Lippy wasn't eating polly seeds, he could really talk.

"I wonder how Margaret O'Brien got discovered," I said.

"It's easier for girls," Brownie said.

Buddy shook his head. "I don't think so. I think it's just a matter of luck, of being in the right place at the right time. What I've got to do is walk around a lot and be seen by all kinds of people. You never can tell when an ordinary person might turn out to be a talent scout. And you never can tell where you'll be discovered. People get discovered in all kinds of places. Like elevators and drugstores."

Buddy might have gone on talking about being discovered forever if Maxie hadn't changed the subject. "So where do we go this afternoon? Luna Park or Steeplechase?"

"I want Luna Park," Brownie answered. "What about you, Lippy?"

"Luna Park," he mumbled.

"That makes two," Brownie said.

"Let Ari be the one who says where we should go," Buddy suggested. "He's the one we're treating, so we should go wherever he wants to."

"What about it, Ari?" Maxie asked. "Luna Park or Steeplechase?"

I was really tempted to say Steeplechase, just to be

different from Brownie. But actually, I like the rides at Luna Park better.

"Luna Park sounds good to me,'" I said. "There's more rides to choose from."

"Okay, that's settled," Maxie said. "Now, how about all of us checking the alleys for empties. We can use some money for food."

"There's nothin' there, I told ya," Brownie said.

"That was yesterday. Somebody must have thrown out a couple of bottles after supper last night. Let's check again."

"While you guys go looking for bottles, I think I'll go change my clothes and clean up," Buddy said. "You never can tell who might be walking around the island."

So while Buddy was making himself even more beautiful, the rest of us went scrounging through the garbage cans, looking for soda bottles. We searched behind all the buildings on Nass Walk. There was plenty of garbage and plenty of flies—but no bottles. Then, when we were just getting ready to leave the alley behind 6–8, Lippy pulled a pair of shoes out of a garbage can. It was a pair of brown crepe-sole shoes, almost new. He held them up in the air. "Look what I . . ."

"Lemme see," said Brownie, and he grabbed the shoes right out of Lippy's hands. "These are nice shoes. I can use 'em."

"Hey, Brownie," Maxie said. "Lippy is the one who found those shoes. Who says you can keep them?"

"Lippy don't want 'em, do you, Lippy?"

"Well . . . I . . ."

"See, I told ya he don't want 'em." Brownie ran out of the alley, yelling, "Ma, Ma, look what I found!"

Lippy just stood there with his mouth open. "It's a good thing that you're not keeping those shoes," I told Lippy. "You never know who wore them. Maybe they belonged to someone who had a contagious disease, and he threw them out when he recovered."

"Yeah," said Maxie. "They didn't look so good to me. They smelled from garbage."

We went back to Nass Walk to wait for Brownie and Buddy. In a few minutes out came Buddy Rizzo, wearing clean dungarees and a polo shirt. And his hair —it wasn't wavy anymore. It was all plastered down and wet-looking. That was it! His hair! Now I knew who he reminded me of. Rudolph Valentino. I saw a photograph of Valentino once—at my Aunt Marilyn's house. Aunt Marilyn told me that he was the only movie star she was ever in love with. And Buddy Rizzo looked just like him.

Pretty soon Brownie came bouncing out, wearing his new brown crepe-sole shoes.

"Hey Brownie," Buddy called. "Where did you get the new shoes?"

"Found 'em," he said, puffing out his fat chest.

"They're very nice," Buddy went on, "but there's one thing wrong with them."

"What's that?"

"They're girls' shoes!" And he slapped his hands on

his thighs and let out this tremendous roar of laughter.

The next thing I knew, Maxie and I were laughing and poking and grabbing each other and practically rolling over in the gutter. Lippy was standing off to the side, laughing into his hand. Brownie was staring at his shoes and turning all shades of red and purple.

When the laughter finally died down, Brownie yelled, "They're not! They're not girls' shoes."

"I'll bet you they are," said Buddy. "If anybody knows about shoes, I do. And I say those are girls' shoes."

"Well, Lippy is the one who really found 'em. You found 'em, Lippy. You want 'em?"

Lippy shook his head. "No thanks, Brownie."

Brownie turned and ran back into his building, yelling, "Ma, Ma!" And boy, did we let loose! Even Lippy. He laughed right out loud this time; he didn't even bother to cover up his face.

When Brownie came out again, he was still wearing the shoes. It seems his mother wasn't about ready to let him throw away a perfectly good pair of shoes that fit him just right—almost.

He gave us all a quick look and said, "Well, what are we standin' around for? Are we goin' to Luna or ain't we?" He started walking up ahead, and then he turned around and waited for us to catch up to him. He looked like he was especially waiting for me. I was right. He pointed to my *yarmulke*. "Do you have to keep wearing that thing?"

"Yes, I do."

"Well, take it off. It bothers me."

"It shouldn't."

"It does. And it bothers Lippy too. Right, Lippy?"

"Right," Lippy said.

"Aw, come on guys," Maxie said. "Quit your arguing. We're going to Coney now. Why spoil everything?"

That's right, I thought. We're going to Coney Island and nobody's going to spoil it. Not even Isidore.

Part of the time we walked along Surf Avenue, but mostly we walked on the boardwalk, tasting the salt air and listening to the clip-clopping of shoes on the wooden boards. The music of the calliopes mingled with the shouts of "Hurry, hurry, walk right up, come and see, come and get, nice and hot, ice cold, guess your weight and win a doll."

We passed fortune-telling gypsies and posters of bearded ladies and fire-eaters. Some of the posters looked fresh and new, while others were torn and tattered—as if they had been hanging there for over a hundred summers.

All around us were the rides. And I love the rides more than anything. I could see the parachute jump at Steeplechase, and the roller coaster rising high above us—the cars clinking and clattering up the track, then dipping and winding, carrying with them the sounds of screaming. The giant ferris wheel was going round and round, sometimes stopping in midair. I wondered what it would feel like to get stuck way up at the top.

With each step we were getting closer and closer to Luna. And even though I had been there many times before, I couldn't remember ever having been so excited. I wanted to shout, "Oh, you rides, wait for me! Luna Park, here I come."

When we finally reached the main entrance, I stopped and waited for the guys to buy the tickets. But they didn't stop. They kept on walking and walking, past the entrance, around a cyclone fence, around some old shacks and around a piece of wooden fence. I ran after them. "Hey you guys. Where's everybody going?"

Maxie swung around and put his finger to his lips. "Sshh." They all kept on walking. At a certain part of the fence, everybody stopped.

"Okay," Maxie said. "One or two at a time. And we meet on the other side."

"Me first," Brownie said. "You come with, Lippy."

Lippy nodded. "Okay."

They sneaked along the fence and turned to see if anyone was watching. Then Brownie lifted up a loose board in the fence and barely, just barely, squeezed himself through. Lippy slipped in afterward.

"Gee, I don't know," I said. "This isn't what I had in mind."

"You didn't really think we were going to *pay* for those rides, did you?" Maxie asked. "Who's got that kind of money?"

"But sneaking in. It's like stealing."

"No it's not," Buddy said. "We're not taking anything

34

from anybody. Lots of people don't get to use up all their rides, and they just throw their tickets away. We'll probably be able to pick up lots of tickets left over from yesterday."

"Yeah," Maxie said. "And if we don't get those tickets, somebody else will. Or they'll get swept up as garbage. Come on. How about it?"

"Well, okay," I said. What else could I say? They were all going, even Lippy. How could I be the only one to say no? And on my second day in the neighborhood too.

"You go first," Maxie told Buddy. "I'll stick with Ari."

"If you think this is hard," Maxie said, "just try to sneak into Steeplechase. They've got a hundred times as many guards around the place. And we never once got caught."

When Buddy disappeared, it was our turn. "If anyone comes," Maxie said, "just say we're looking for the men's room."

We crept along the fence. My heart was thumping so loudly, I wondered if Maxie could hear it. I wished I was back on Rivington Street. I wished I had never heard of Nass Walk or Maxie Friedman.

When we reached the loose board, Maxie swung it to the side, stuck his head through the fence and crawled in. I glanced around a few times and started in after him. When we reached the other side, Maxie said, "See, nothing to it."

We found Brownie, Lippy and Buddy searching the

ground for the heart-shaped tickets that didn't have all the ride numbers punched out. We joined the search. To me it seemed like we spent half the morning looking for rides. But we found some good ones: The Mile Sky Chaser, Chute-the-Chutes and The Dragon's Gorge. According to Brownie, a lot of people use up the sissy rides and throw the best ones away.

My favorite ride is the Chutes. You go up something like an elevator in a boat. Then the boat comes sliding down a wet, slippery slide—fast! And splash! Right into the water. You get soaking wet, but it feels great on a hot day.

The Mile Sky Chaser is a scary roller-coaster ride that's only fun when it's over. And The Dragon's Gorge is a spooky roller-coaster ride in pitch blackness. For me it's the most frightening ride in the park. Just the thought of it is enough to send shivers all up and down my spine.

I thought about it while the guys were searching for tickets, and suddenly the whole park felt spooky to me. I walked over to Maxie and crouched down beside him. "You know, Maxie, I've got a funny feeling about what we're doing. Like somebody's inside me, trying to warn us about something. Let's go."

"Aw, your conscience is botherin' ya," said Brownie, as he examined a ticket and threw it away. "I seen it in the movies lots of times. A devil sits on one shoulder, tellin' ya to do somethin' bad, and an angel sits on your other shoulder, tellin' ya not to do it."

"It only looks like that in the movies," Buddy said.

"There isn't any devil or angel sitting on anyone's shoulder."

"Well, maybe it is my conscience," I said. "And maybe it's telling us to get out of here before something happens."

"Come on," said Maxie. "Quit your worrying and help us look for some more rides."

Right then and there I should have left. But it wasn't the easiest thing to walk out on guys I expected to be friends with. I figured the sooner I could find us some rides to go on, the sooner we could leave. So there I was, looking around and not having much luck, when a voice from above shouted, "Okay, what do you kids think you're doing here?"

We scrambled to our feet. A fat park guard was standing next to us. Sweat was dripping down his face. "I asked you a question. What are you doing here?"

"We're looking for the men's room," I stammered. He started to laugh—a mean kind of laugh.

"Let's get out of here!" Maxie shouted.

"Run for your life!" Buddy hollered.

The guard blew his whistle, Brownie yelled, "Charge!" and we took off. We raced through the park, in and out of ticket lines, knocking into people, dodging around refreshment stands and kiddy rides. We leaped over ropes and crashed through gates, pushing and shoving anyone and anything that got in our way. And all the while, the whistle was sounding right behind us.

"Hurry, this way," Maxie called, motioning to us

with a wave of his hand. We scooted around a corner and ducked into The Hall of Mirrors. We found a small, dark passageway and huddled there, panting. "There's another way out of here," Maxie said in between breaths. "At the other end of the passageways. Let's go!"

We ran through the maze of distorted mirrors. All five of us, squatty, pear-shaped, upside-down fugitives. We ran and ran. Finally we burst out of the last passageway and ran through the park until we reached the main gate. Then we nonchalantly walked out of the park and down the narrow street that led back to the boardwalk.

"Well, at least you got your wish," I said to Buddy as we were walking. "You got discovered at the island."

"I got my wish too," Brownie added.

"You didn't tell me you had a wish," Lippy said. "What was it?"

"I wished for a way to get rid of those damn shoes."

We looked down at Brownie's stocking feet, and he wiggled his toes. "I guess I must've run right out of 'em." Then he yelled, "Charge!" And we raced off toward the beach.

5

"What we need is money," Maxie said.

We were sitting on the fire escape, eating Sunkist navel oranges and throwing the peels down into the yard.

"If we would've had money the other day, we never would've gotten into all that trouble at Luna Park."

"Trouble is right," I said. "More things have been happening these last few days than have ever happened to me in my whole life. First that lady under the boardwalk, and then Luna Park. When do things ever get normal around here?"

"Heck, Ari. This *is* normal. You'll soon find out there's always something doing around here. You'll love living on Nass Walk. And if you take my advice, you'll get rid of the beanie. You'll fit in a lot better with us if you do."

"But I always wear my *yarmulke*, Maxie."

"For Pete's sake. What for?"

"All Jews who observe the tradition wear them. I observe, so I wear one. All my friends on the East Side do."

"But you're not on the East Side now. You're in Brooklyn."

"Guys in Brooklyn wear them too."

"Not on Nass Walk, they don't. Anyway, it's just a suggestion. What I really want to talk about is how we can earn some money. You can't move around here without a few cents in your pocket. What if we want to go see Tarzan when it comes, or rent bikes and ride to Prospect Park, or hop a subway uptown, or we're walking along Brighton and get in the mood for egg creams? We've got to make some money."

"I made a few cents last summer," I told Maxie. "I used to watch the neighbors' kids when the mothers went shopping."

"Well, that won't work around here," he said. "There's not a mother on this whole block who'll trust me with her kids. Anyway, I've got a better idea. You and I are going into business."

"What kind of business?"

"The shoe shine business."

"You mean we'll become shoe shine boys?"

"Yeah. Jack did it last year and made a fortune."

"Who's Jack?"

"Brownie's brother."

"I didn't know he had a brother."

"How could you miss him? He pretty darn near wakes up the whole neighborhood every morning with that trumpet of his."

"Oh, so he's the one. He sure plays a lousy trumpet."

"Yeah. Well, anyway, last year he went shoe shining. His mother almost killed him when she found out. She didn't think it was nice for a Jewish boy to shine shoes. But he made a fortune."

"I don't think my mother would be too crazy about the idea either," I said.

"And I know for sure my ma would have a fit if I did it. But who says they ever have to find out? All we do is go out and buy some polish and a few brushes, and we're in business. This time *we'll* make the fortune."

"Great idea," I said. "But where do we get the money to buy the polish and brushes so we can go into business and make a fortune?"

Maxie nodded. "Yeah. That's the problem."

Then from the roof we heard Benjy crying, "Breathe! Breathe! You're not breathing! Why don't you breathe?"

"Oh, oh," Maxie said, as he jumped to his feet. "Sounds like something's happened to Benjy's pigeons."

We made a mad dash for the roof. Benjy was in the corner, struggling with his pigeons, trying to press their beaks together. "Breathe! Breathe!" he cried.

"What's going on?" Maxie called.

"They won't breathe, Maxie. All week I've tried to breathe them like Ari told me. But they won't breathe."

Maxie let out a howl. "You're not supposed to *breathe* them, dopey. You *breed* them. B-R-E-E-D.

Breed." And he laughed so hard, I thought he'd fall off the roof.

Benjy put the pigeons back into the coop and turned away. "You know something," I said to him. "I used to think the same thing. Whenever my father used the word *breed*, I always thought he said *breathe*."

Benjy looked up at me. "Really?"

"Sure," I said. "I bet lots of kids think that."

Maxie stopped laughing. He came over and put his hand on Benjy's shoulder. "Sure, dopey," he said. "I would've thought the same thing at your age."

"Okay," Benjy said, "how do I *breed* my pigeons?"

"Just keep them together a lot," I said. "It might happen by itself."

A wide smile spread across Benjy's face. "Gee, that's even easier than breathing," he said.

"What a crazy kid," Maxie said.

We sat on the fire escape and did some more thinking about our shoe shining business.

"You know," I said after a while, "maybe we're going about this thing all wrong. Maybe instead of buying the equipment we need, we can borrow it. A little polish here, a couple of brushes there, and we're all set."

"Borrow from who?" Maxie asked.

"Our fathers, for instance."

"I don't think that would work," Maxie said. "My father doesn't even have polish. He wipes his shoes on his pants when they get dusty. And if they're real

43

dirty, he washes them with a wet towel. And besides, if we borrow polish from anyone we know, our mothers will find out, and we'll get killed."

"I forgot about that," I said. "I guess we'll have to buy the stuff after all."

Our thoughts were interrupted by shouts from below. From where we were sitting on the fire escape, we could see real good. The super was down in the yard, picking up orange peels. Pretty soon he was shaking his fist and yelling at us in a foreign language. I figured it was probably Greek, because that's what the super was—Greek. We couldn't understand what he was saying, but one word came out loud and clear. It was a word we would soon be used to hearing—in many languages. And in any language it always came out the same. Bums! We heard it and ran.

As soon as I reached the safety of my apartment, I forgot all about the super and remembered it was Friday.

Friday is like no other day in the week. My mother had the freshly washed floors covered with newspapers, and I could smell the chicken and soup cooking on the stove and the *challah* baking in the oven. My mother always bakes her own *challah*. Even with bakeries close by, and even though my Aunt Marilyn keeps telling her it's old-fashioned to bake bread when you can buy it ready-made.

My mother poured me a glass of milk and cut me a piece of coffee cake. "A new recipe," she said. "Mrs.

Silverman told me it's hard to miss with it." She scooped up a few crumbs from the table and started nibbling. Then she laughed. "You know something? I think I missed."

"It's not bad, Ma," I said. I sat there, eating and drinking, and found myself staring at the *pushkes* on the window sill. Ever since I can remember, the *pushkes* were always on our kitchen window sill. There are three of them: the blue-and-white box with the Star of David on the front, for planting trees in Palestine; the yellow box for orphans in Palestine; and the brown one for the poor, right here in New York City.

Sometimes I thought it strange to be giving money to the poor, when we didn't have much ourselves. I asked my mother about it once. She told me it was considered one of the greatest deeds in Judaism to give charity. "A great *mitzvah*," she said. "Because no matter how little we have, there are always those who have less."

And every Friday night that I can remember, before the Sabbath, before my mother would light the candles, she would drop pennies, nickels or dimes into each of the boxes. Every so often, bearded men with long black coats and black hats would come to collect the money. I remember, when I was little, the way they came and pinched my cheek and smiled at me.

There's sort of a fourth charity box on the window sill. Actually, it's just a metal tea can that my mother uses to save up money for emergencies or for a "little something." It's red and gold, and it looks like a treasure chest. There's a slot cut in the lid. We call it Mama's *pushke*, but she hardly ever uses the money to buy things for herself, except her yearly hat. Every year she buys a crazy hat with a crazy feather for the High Holidays in fall. She wears the hat all year to the synagogue on Saturdays, and the next year she treats herself to a new one. But mostly she'll spend the money on a book for my father or a model-airplane kit for me to put together when I'm sick. Once, just once, she "threw out" a dime to buy me a Superman comic book when I had the chicken pox.

All these things I was thinking about and remembering over my cake and milk.

"Is something wrong?" my mother asked.

"No, nothing," I said. "I was just thinking how certain things always stay the same. Fridays in Brooklyn feel just like Fridays on the East Side. Nothing's changed. I guess they'd be the same for us everywhere."

"Everywhere? No, Ari, not everywhere. If we were living in Europe, they wouldn't be the same for us. Not with that maniac Hitler running around." That faraway look came back to her eyes.

It was still there when my father came home from work. "Malkeh again?" he asked.

"No," I said. "This time it was me."

Later my mother dropped some coins into the *pushkes*, and my father set out to look for a new synagogue. By the time he came home, my mother had the table set with the white linen tablecloth. The candles were burning in the silver candlesticks, and next to the candlesticks were the two loaves of *challah* and the goblet filled with the wine that I myself had chosen, just before Passover, from the many barrels at Schapiro's.

"Good *Shabbos*," my father said and kissed my mother on the cheek. He placed his hand on my head and blessed me, "May God make thee as Ephraim and Manasseh." Then he chanted the *kiddush* over the wine.

We ate our Sabbath meal of gefilte fish and soup and roast meat with *tzimmes*, and when we were finished, my mother poured us each some tea. We drank it the way Aunt Marilyn whole-heartedly disapproves of, a very old-fashioned, un-American way. In glasses.

A gentle summer breeze blew in from the kitchen window. It rustled the curtains and made the candles flicker. I stared into the candlelight and listened to my father sing the Sabbath songs. Then I sang too.

The next morning I walked to the synagogue on West Third Street with my father. I was a little nervous about going to a new place and hoped that Maxie would be there, so I could sit next to him.

When we walked into the synagogue, we could hear an old man chanting a prayer.

"Let's sit in the back, where we won't be noticed," I whispered. My father smiled, but he kept on walking up the aisle toward the ark. All kinds of heads turned around to look at us. But none of them belonged to Maxie. The rabbi smiled at us as we sat down.

All during the services I kept turning around toward the door, looking for Maxie. One time I saw my mother walk in with her crazy hat.

"Why is the back of the *shul* so much more interesting than the front?" my father asked in his quiet synagogue voice.

"I'm looking for Maxie."

"Maybe he goes to a different *shul*."

"I never thought of that," I said.

By the middle of the service, when I gave up on Maxie, I started to pay attention to what was going on in front of me. I listened as the men were called up to read from the Torah, and I watched as the Torah was carried in procession throughout the synagogue. When it came to us, my father and I drew close to it and he touched it with his prayer shawl.

For a moment I felt like I was back on the East Side again. The people were different, but everything else, the melodies and the ceremonies, was the same. I guess they've always been the same—for hundreds and hundreds of years—and probably always will be.

Then, because I was new to the synagogue, I was asked to sing *"Adon Olam"* at the end of the service. It is a hymn that I've sung many times before, and I know it by heart. So I sang—just as some other boy might have sung it almost a thousand years ago.

אֲדוֹו עוֹלָם אֲשֶׁר מָלַךְ · · ·

He is the eternal Lord who reigned
Before any being was created.
. . . He is without beginning, without end.

When it was all over, the rabbi and the old man who chanted the prayers came up to tell me that I had a fine voice and I'd make a great cantor. Funny, that's what everybody on the East Side always told me. I think I'd like that—to be a cantor.

I walked home with my mother and father. My mother's hat had a battered, beat-up look. I thought it would make a perfect nest for Benjy's pigeons.

"It looks like you'll be needing that new hat pretty soon, Ma," I said.

"No, Ari. There will be no new hat this year. I'll make do with the one I have."

"Sarah, am I hearing right?" my father asked. "No new hat? It's not like you to break such a tradition."

"There are more important things than hats, Abe. I didn't mention anything about it before, but this year I've been saving for something special. A trip to Chicago to see my sister Leah. It's been too long since we've seen each other. Much too long. So no new hat. A new feather maybe, just a new feather."

"You could get a feather from one of Benjy's pigeons," I suggested.

My mother smiled and said, "That's not what I had in mind."

As we approached our building, I saw Buddy sitting

on the curb, shaving off the bark of a branch with a scout knife.

"Hi, Buddy," I called.

"Hi, Ari."

My mother shook her head. "How can a boy play with a knife on a day like today? And look! He isn't dressed up for *Shabbos*."

"Why should he be?" I asked. "He isn't even Jewish." And I ran into the building to look for Maxie.

6

I found Maxie and Benjy up on the roof, eating watermelon. Maxie was spitting the seeds over the wall.

"You bum you!" I called, as I stepped onto the roof. "What's going on here? First it's orange peels, now it's watermelon seeds." I shook my fist at him.

"Oh hi, Ari. I'm planting watermelon. Have some." He handed me a slice. Mrs. Friedman cut it thick—the way she did the salami and bread. I took a bite of that sweet, delicious melon and tried to spit out a seed like Maxie did. It landed on my chin.

"I didn't see you at services today," I told Maxie.

"Maybe that's because I wasn't there."

"Yeah. I figured you probably went to a different synagogue."

"Well, you figured wrong. I don't go to any of them. I like to sleep late on Saturday mornings and fool around afterward. How about you? You go often?"

"I've gone practically every Saturday of my life," I said. And I told Maxie about the cantor that sang at our synagogue on the East Side, and the beautiful voice he had, and how I used to like to go and listen to him sing.

"I went to services a couple of times," Maxie said. "But to me it's just a bunch of old men standing around, saying a lot of things in Hebrew that I can't understand. What's the sense of going when you can't even understand what they're saying?"

"You sound like my Aunt Marilyn," I told him. "She says she doesn't see any point in going to a service that's in a language she can't understand. But she thinks it's very classy to go to the opera, and she doesn't know a word of Italian."

I spit out another seed. It slid down the front of my neck.

"Hey, you're doing that all wrong," Maxie said. "You've got to keep your mouth and tongue in just the right position. Like this." And he shot a seed practically across the yard.

"What about Hebrew School?" I asked. "Which one do you go to?"

"None of them," he said. "I quit Hebrew when I moved here from Brownsville. It was too much like work. I'd quit public school too, if there wasn't a law saying I had to go. My ma was all upset about it for a while. But Benjy goes now, so she's satisfied."

Benjy was trying to feed his pigeons some watermelon seeds. He wasn't having much luck.

"I think they like peanuts better," he said.

"Watch it, dopey," Maxie said. "You keep doing that and your pigeons will be giving birth to watermelons."

"I just thought of something," I said to Maxie. "If

you're not going to Hebrew, how can you get ready for your *Bar Mitzvah*?"

"I can't. And who cares? Why all the fuss just because a guy gets to be thirteen years old?"

I was pretty surprised by what he said because most guys look forward to their *Bar Mitzvah*. I know I do.

A *Bar Mitzvah* marks the time you first get to be called up to read from the Torah and participate in the services like an adult. In fact, from then on, you're treated like an adult in all religious matters. You have a special celebration and get presents too. But you're not supposed to care about that part. I guess Maxie didn't care about any part of it.

He finished eating and started to wipe his mouth on Benjy's shirt.

"Hey, cut it out!" Benjy cried.

"There's *one* thing I'll miss about not having a *Bar Mitzvah*," Maxie said.

"What's that? The presents?"

"No. My speech. I'd like to have a *Bar Mitzvah* speech and say, 'And to my dear Aunt Minnie, thank you for the fountain pen. It should only run from your nose like it runs from your pen.'" With that he let out a howl.

"That's an old, old joke," I said.

"Yeah, but it's a good one."

Just then the big steel door opened, and Brownie and Lippy walked onto the roof. They were each sipping syrup from a tiny bottle made of wax.

54

"Whatcha guys doin'?" Brownie asked.

"Nothing much," Maxie answered. "What about you?"

Brownie popped the whole wax bottle into his mouth and began chewing. "Me and Lippy were thinking of taking the subway uptown."

"To watch Buddy get discovered," Lippy said, and he popped his bottle into his mouth too.

"It's too hot to go all the way up there today," Maxie said. "Let's go for a ride on the trolley cars."

"Sounds okay," Brownie said, and he spit the wad of wax over the wall. "Is it okay with you, Lippy?"

"Sure," Lippy said and spit his wad of wax out too. It landed on his chin.

If there was one thing I wouldn't do, it would be to go riding around in a trolley car on a Saturday. "I'll see you guys later," I said. "I'm going in for lunch."

"Okay," Maxie said. "And after you finish, get out of your monkey suit, put on some regular clothes and come on with us."

"Not today, thanks," I said, and I went down to my apartment. My mother and father were already sitting at the table, waiting for me.

I like the way our house feels on the Sabbath. I like the way we can sit around the table long after we've finished eating, and talk and laugh and sing the Sabbath songs. It's the one day in the week my mother can relax and read and visit with her friends and wear a nice dress. There's no cleaning, no shopping, no cooking. In the summer we eat cold foods, and in the winter we eat hot *cholent*, a stew of meat, potatoes and lima beans, prepared on Friday and slow-cooked over a low flame all through the night and past the early morning hours.

My mother calls the Sabbath her "Day of Delight." The Sabbath is my father's "Day of Delight" too. He doesn't have to go to work and sit over his sewing machine all day. He can spend the day at home and in the synagogue. Every Sabbath he goes to the synagogue in the morning to pray, and again, in the afternoon, to learn and discuss the Bible and Talmud— Jewish philosophy and law—with the other men. He has done this practically every Saturday of his life— every Saturday that I can remember.

Once I asked, "Don't you ever get tired of learning all the time?"

"There's beauty and knowledge in those books, Ari. A person can never tire of beauty and knowledge."

"But don't you know it all by now?"

"A person can study the Bible and Talmud his entire life and never learn it all."

Even today he was talking about finding a new synagogue to learn in, now that we're no longer on the East Side.

"I hear that a small group of men meet every *Shabbos* over on Seabreeze Avenue. I think I'll try it there today. Why don't you come by later, Ari? We'll walk home together."

After lunch I went out into the street. Nass Walk was still and quiet. None of the guys were around. Probably riding in a trolley car somewhere, I supposed, and for the second time I wished that I were back on the Lower East Side again. Back with my friends, spending the Sabbath together the way we always did—visiting each other's homes or spending an afternoon at Seward Park.

I took a walk around the neighborhood and saw the streets alive with other Sabbath strollers. As they passed, they wished me, "Good *Shabbos*."

"Good *Shabbos*," I wished them back.

I walked over to the park on Seabreeze Avenue and then across the street to the synagogue where my father was learning. The men were sitting at a long table in the main sanctuary, engaged in friendly argument. Voices were rising and falling, sometimes speaking all at once and sometimes one at a time. The men were discussing the sage Hillel and interpreting his saying, "If I am not for myself, who will be for me? And if I am only for myself, what am I?"

I always thought the saying meant that you have to care about yourself because if you don't, who will? But at the same time you have to care about other people too. I couldn't see what there was to discuss.

I listened for a while and went over to another long table, where I helped myself to some *kichel* and a small cup of wine. A short time later my father joined me and introduced me to his new friends.

When we left the synagogue, I asked, "Why all the discussion about that saying of Hillel's? Doesn't it mean just what it says?"

"The meaning goes deeper than the words, Ari," he said.

We started to cross Seabreeze Avenue and stopped to let a trolley go by. And that's when I saw them. All three of them. Maxie, Brownie and Lippy, hitching onto the back of the trolley. They saw me and yelled, "Hey, Ari!"

I laughed and waved to them. "You guys are crazy," I shouted. Then my father and I walked home together.

7

"I almost split my head open," Maxie said, pointing to the bandage on his forehead. We were working on model airplanes in my kitchen on Monday, and he was telling me the story for about the tenth time.

"I just lost my grip and fell off the trolley," he went on. "I still can't understand how that happened. I've been riding on the backs of trolley cars for years now, and this was the first time I ever fell off one. Lucky for me, those cops were around to get me to Coney Island Hospital. You should've seen us speeding along, siren and all. They were even nice enough to bring my mother over so she could sign papers saying it was all right for me to get stitched up. I was just lucky I didn't split my head open."

"Well, you sure had everybody scared to death," I said. And he did too. About an hour after my father and I returned from the synagogue, we heard Mrs. Friedman scream in the hallway. The police had come to take her to her son, who, according to Brownie and

59

Lippy, was dying of a severe head wound and loss of blood.

Practically everybody in the building went outside to wait for Mrs. Friedman to come home with news of Maxie. Were we ever relieved when he came back with her, very much alive and wearing only a small bandage on his forehead.

"You can't imagine how happy I was to see you getting out of that cab," I told him. "And walking on your own two feet."

"Yeah. I was glad to be walking too. And thanks again for the plane."

"It was the least I could do." Making model airplanes is my hobby. And I had given Maxie a P-38 as a welcome-home present.

Maxie wasn't able to concentrate on his plane, and he started walking around the kitchen. "I see your ma keeps her *pushkes* on the window sill," he said. "That's where my ma keeps hers."

"I guess everyone does."

"What's this?" he asked, pointing to the tea can.

"That's my mother's private *pushke*," I answered.

He lifted the can. "It sure is heavy. I bet she's got a fortune in here."

I had to laugh at that. "Some fortune. It's mostly pennies, nickels and dimes. A few quarters maybe."

"You know something, Ari. I think all our problems are solved."

I wished he'd stop talking so I could concentrate on

the wing I was trimming. "What do you mean?" I asked.

Maxie held up the can. "The money we need—to buy the shoe shine stuff . . ."

I jumped up from my chair and almost cut myself with the razor blade. "Oh no we don't! I'm not about to steal money from my own mother."

As I said that word—steal—I could practically see Moses standing on top of Mount Sinai with the Ten Commandments, pointing to the eighth one—Thou shalt not steal.

"Oh no. Not me. Forget it."

"Don't get so dramatic," Maxie said. "You're not stealing anything. You're just . . . borrowing. Just a couple of dollars. You'll be able to put it back before she'll even know it's missing. More even. Shoe shining is a fantastic business. We'll make five times as much in one day."

I started to think about that. Five times as much in one day. I could just picture it. My mother opening her tea can and seeing all that money. And I would say, "It's yours, Ma, every cent of it. Go out and buy that new hat. Buy ten new hats. And a new coat. Buy anything you want. And you don't have to wait for that trip to Chicago. You can go today. Right now." I could just picture me saying all that.

"Are you sure, Maxie? Are you sure we can make all that money?"

"Sure, I'm sure. I told you about Jack, didn't I?"

"Okay, I'll do it, tonight after supper. When they go outside."

We cleaned up the mess on the kitchen table and went out to look for a wooden box. We found a good one behind Springer's Fruit Store. We carried the box to the alley behind 2–4, and Maxie ran into the building to borrow the super's tools.

"I know just how to do it," Maxie said, as he began to rip the box apart. "I saw the box Jack made last year. Nothing to it."

Maxie went wild. He banged, ripped, sawed and hammered. I hated to think what he'd be doing to that P-38. He was finished in no time at all. "Well, how do you like it?" he asked.

It wasn't the most beautiful-looking box in the world, but it had storage space and just enough room on top for a foot.

"You sure finished in a hurry," I said.

He grinned. "I don't fool around."

"Maybe we should have two boxes," I suggested. "We can work twice as fast that way."

"We'll have enough trouble hiding one box without having to worry about two."

We brought the tools back to the basement and then tried to figure out where to hide the box.

"I'll keep it under my bed," Maxie said after a while.

"What if your ma finds it?"

"She won't. She just cleaned under there on Friday, so she won't get to it for another six months or so.

Anyway, it's the least I can do. You're getting the money; I'll hide the box."

I had a hard time eating supper that night. I was so nervous, I kept looking at the tea can and seeing Moses.

After my mother finished the dishes, she and my father got ready to go out and sit with the neighbors. That's what they like to do on hot nights—either sit with the neighbors or go with them for walks around the block.

"Aren't you coming out tonight, Ari?" My mother asked.

"No. I think I'll stay in and work on my plane . . . or something."

"I'll keep you company," my father said.

"No, Pa. You don't have to do that. I'll be down in a while." I practically pushed him out the door.

After they left, I stood in front of the tea can, staring at it. My hands started sweating and my throat felt dry. Something deep inside me told me not to do it. But I did it anyway. I lifted the lid and grabbed a fistful of coins: pennies, nickels, dimes and quarters—whatever there was. I didn't bother to look, to think, to count. The minute I took the money, I was sorry I did it. Maybe I could put it back. Maybe there was still time. But then I heard a noise at the door. It was too late.

I ran to my room, threw myself on the bed and looked up at the ceiling. And suddenly I knew I wasn't alone. Someone was watching me. Up there someone saw everything I did. He knew. Would He understand? I waited for a bolt of lightning to come out of the heavens and strike me down. But nothing happened.

8

""Two dollars and eleven cents," I told Maxie. We were in the alley, counting the money. I couldn't even bear to look at it the night before. When my folks came up from outside, I pretended to be asleep because I couldn't bear to look at them either.

"Come on, Maxie. Let's get going. I've got to get that money back in the can today."

"Relax. All we've got to do is make one stop at Woolworth's, and we're on our way."

We went over to Brighton Beach Avenue and bought whatever Maxie thought we'd need—a can of black polish and a can of brown, some shoe wash, a couple of brushes and a metal footrest. Maxie brought rags from home. The whole thing came to a little over two dollars.

When we got out of the store, Maxie took a screwdriver and four screws—compliments of the super—from his pocket and attached the footrest to the top of the box.

"There! We're all set."

I was impressed. "Boy, you sure have everything planned."

"I told you. I don't fool around."

"Where to now?" I asked, anxious to get started.

"Surf Avenue. It'll be mobbed. We'll catch the guys just as they come off the boardwalk with sand on their shoes." Then Maxie reached up and took the *yarmulke* off my head. "Here," he said. "You'd better put this away. Jewish boys aren't supposed to shine shoes, remember?"

I took the *yarmulke* and stuck it in my pocket.

As Maxie predicted, Surf Avenue was packed. We ran after every guy who looked like he could afford five cents for a shine.

I'd walk up to a guy and ask, "Would you like a shine, sir?" Get that—sir. Well, he'd just walk away like he never even heard me. I'm some salesman. But Maxie, he really hustled.

"Shine, mister? Shoes look a little dusty. Only a nickel and they'll look like new." The guy would look at his dusty shoes and nod, and we'd get ourselves a customer.

We got six customers that day, and we took turns shining. One guy gave us a dime, and he didn't even look rich. Shining shoes was sure an easy way to make money.

After a while Maxie said, "Hey Ari. Let's go get a couple of franks at Nathan's. All this work is making me hungry."

"We can't spend this money," I told him. "I've got

66

to put it back in the tea can. And besides, Nathan's isn't kosher."

"Oh that. I forgot. Well, we can go to a Hebrew National stand if you want. And don't worry about the money. You saw how easy it was to get it. We'll get some more later."

The smells from all that food were getting to me again just like they did that first day on the boardwalk. "Well, okay. I'm kind of hungry too. As long as we can make some more later on."

We bought some kosher franks and french fries and a couple of Cokes. When we were all through eating, we were too full and too tired to do any more shining. There's always tomorrow, we told ourselves. One more day wouldn't make any difference, would it?

Nobody wants their shoes shined in the rain. And that's what we had for the next three days—rain. And for the next three days I was a wreck. I hardly slept. And when I was awake, I kept my eyes on the tea can all day, hoping my mother wouldn't decide it was time to count her money. She doesn't do it often. She says that too much counting is like watching a pot of soup on the stove. It won't boil.

On Saturday my mother woke me up for services. I felt too rotten to go. Too rotten to do anything but stay in bed. "I want to sleep," I said to my mother without looking at her.

"But it's *Shabbos*, Ari. You'll be late for *shul*." She put her hand on my forehead. "Are you sick?"

"No, I'm okay. I just want to sleep late on Saturday for a change—to see what it's like."

"I suppose it's all right. There's no crime in it."

I practically jumped out of bed. "Crime? What do you mean?"

"Ari, what's the matter with you? I just mean that it's all right for you to stay in bed if you feel like it. I don't know, you've been acting so strange lately." She walked out of the room, shaking her head.

I heard a little mumbling coming from the kitchen. A few minutes later my father came into the room and sat on my bed. I couldn't look at him either.

"Ari, is there something you want to tell me?"

I swallowed hard. "What should I want to tell you?"

"I don't know. I thought . . . well . . . I'll see you when I come home from *shul*." He got up and walked out.

I couldn't go back to sleep, so I got up, got dressed, and fixed myself some Wheaties. Then I went out to look for Maxie. He wasn't on the roof, and he wasn't in the street, so I figured he was still in bed. None of the other guys were out, so I walked over to the park and watched some old men playing checkers. Then I went back to Nass Walk.

Maxie and the others were sitting on the curb, talking. Maxie got up when he saw me. "Hi Ari. I thought you'd be at services as usual."

"I didn't go. I felt like sleeping late today."

He slapped me on the back. "Good boy. You learn

fast. Just stick with old Maxie. I'll turn you into an All-American Boy yet." The other guys smiled at him when he said that.

"I thought I already was one," I said.

"Not with this on your head, you're not." He took the *yarmulke* off and dangled it in front of me. I pulled it away from him and stuck it back on.

Just then Maxie's mother stuck her head out of the window and started hollering. "Maxie, come up here!"

"Later, Ma. We're having an important discussion."

"Don't give me any laters, Maxie. You come up this minute."

Maxie pulled me off to the side. "We're in trouble. I think she found the box."

"But I thought she wouldn't be cleaning under your bed for another six months."

"Yeah. That's what I thought too. She'll kill me when I get up there."

"Well, good luck," I said.

"What do you mean, good luck? You're coming with me."

"Oh no I'm not. If I wanted to get yelled at I would've hidden the box under *my* bed."

"Boy, some pal you turned out to be. Aw, come on, Ari. My ma likes you. She'll be easier on me if you're there. You don't have to say anything. Just stand there next to me."

"Well, okay. I guess things can't get much worse than they already are."

All the way up the stairs, Maxie was mumbling, "We're done for. Finished. This is the end."

Then all of a sudden it hit me. Without that shoe shine box, how would I ever make the money to put back into the tea can?

Mrs. Friedman was waiting for us at the top of the stairs with her hands on her hips. She pointed to the door. "Inside." Once we were in, she quietly closed the door, looked at Maxie and very calmly said, "I have something to tell you."

She had such a serious expression on her face, I wondered if somebody died. "Maxie," she went on, "somebody stole Mrs. Silverman's bloomers."

Well, Maxie and I let out whoops of laughter like you've never heard before. "That could be pretty rough on Mrs. Silverman," Maxie said, clutching his side.

"Maxie!" Mrs. Friedman shouted.

"Especially in the winter."

"Maxie!"

"I hope she's got another pair."

By this time we were almost rolling across the floor.

"Stop that laughing. Both of you!" Mrs. Friedman shouted. "Tell me, Maxie. Did you take Mrs. Silverman's bloomers from the line?"

Maxie collapsed on a chair and dried his eyes.

"*Nu*, Maxie? I'm waiting."

"Aw Ma, come on. What would I want with an old pair of ladies' bloomers?"

"I don't know, Maxie. But first Mrs. Plotkin tells me

what you were looking for under the boardwalk . . ."

"That snitcher."

"And now Mrs. Silverman says you took her bloomers."

"Of course she'd say that," Maxie burst out. "She hates me. Whenever something goes wrong around here, she says, 'Maxie did it!'" He raised his voice about five octaves in imitation of Mrs. Silverman.

Maxie got up and walked over to me. "Gee, Ari, you should've been here last winter. The super forgot to turn the heat up one day, and Mrs. Silverman said I sabotaged the furnace."

He turned to his mother. "She blames everything on me. I bet if you ask her who started World War II, she'll say Maxie did it. Go ahead, Ma, ask her. Ask her who started World War II."

"All right, all right," Mrs. Friedman said. "Sha already. I believe you. I believe you about the bloomers. But what about Mrs. Plotkin?"

"Mrs. Plotkin is a nosey old lady," he said, as he threw open the door and stormed out of the apartment. "Wait till I get my hands on the guy who did it."

"Maybe nobody did it," I said. "Maybe the bloomers just blew off the roof."

"I've been framed, I tell you."

We started down the stairs, and just before we reached the door of the apartment building, I stopped and said, "Say, Maxie, tell me something. I'd like to know . . . why *did* you start World War II?"

"Very funny," he said, and we went out into the street. Maxie ran across the gutter, yelling, "Okay, which one of you guys did it?"

"Did what?" Brownie asked.

"You know what I mean. Who's going around stealing underwear?"

"Not me," Brownie said. "I've got enough of my own."

"Me too," said Lippy.

"What about you, Buddy?" Maxie asked.

"Not lately," he said, laughing. "Why? Whose underwear is missing?"

"None of your business," Maxie said. "And you guys better be telling the truth. I don't like getting blamed for something I didn't do."

"I still say they blew off the roof," I told Maxie.

Then from up above there came a shout. "Look out below!" This time Benjy was the one who was sticking his head out the window. And floating out of the sky was Benjy's parachute.

"Oh no, it can't be!" Maxie hollered.

"It is!" I yelled. "And it's pink."

"And it's got strings."

"Isn't it a swell parachute?" Benjy called.

Maxie caught the parachute and held it up. "Yeah, it sure is swell, all right." And he ran into the building.

A few minutes later I heard a voice from way up on the roof, and I looked up to see the parachute flying right out of the sky. "It's a bird. It's a plane. It's . . ."

"A pair of bloomers!" Brownie shouted, as he and the others ran around, trying to catch it.

We watched the parachute sail through the air until it landed on the nearby telephone wires. Mrs. Silverman's bloomers looked so crazy sitting there that we all burst out laughing. I was laughing so hard, I almost missed seeing my mother and father walking back from the synagogue.

For the first time in my life I had forgotten the Sabbath.

9

On Monday I took my *yarmulke* off again and went shoe shining with Maxie. Business was pretty good on Surf Avenue, but Maxie said it would be even better uptown. So we walked over to Brighton Beach Avenue, stopped at a candy store for egg creams and hopped a subway to Manhattan. We took the Brighton Express all the way to Forty-second Street.

Boy, the Forty-second–Street station is really something! I said to Maxie, "There's a whole world right here under the ground. Food, bathrooms, shops. Everything a person needs to survive. You could live here forever without having to come up for air."

"Not me," he said. "I'd feel like a prisoner down here. I need my freedom."

We tried to pick up a little business in the station, but people just rushed past us as if we didn't even exist. Outside it was a real nothing too. We couldn't get anyone to look at us. People were running in a million different directions. "I think the only way to get people to notice us is to run around naked."

"Yeah. We'll just wear shoes."

"Yeah. Real clean and shiny."

Boy, was it ever hot! We were dripping with sweat. So we stopped for a couple of Nedicks orange drinks, making sure we'd each have a nickel left for the subway back.

The drinks went down cold and fast. Then some guy came up and asked us for a shine. Just like that. Maxie took the right foot, and when he finished, I took the left. He gave us each a nickel. Our drinks were gone, but we hung around the stand anyway, just in case somebody else would want a shine. But that guy was the only one.

We headed up Forty-second Street and walked up and down some of the avenues. We were getting used to the crowds now, and we rushed right along with everybody, stopping people whenever we could, and trying to convince them that they needed shines. In all that time, about two hours, we only made twenty cents. And we blew the whole thing on egg creams because we were so thirsty.

I was so disgusted with the whole day, I just wanted to go home. Even Maxie lost his usual spirit. "We should've stayed in Brooklyn," he said.

We took the subway back to Brighton Beach Avenue and sneaked home through the alley so nobody would see the shoe shine box. I told Maxie I would meet him on the roof after supper.

My mother nearly fainted when she saw me. "Ari, you look terrible. Where were you all day?"

"Out walking with Maxie," I said, flopping into a kitchen chair.

"In this heat?"

"We didn't realize it would be this hot when we started out."

I saw my mother's eyes rest on the top of my head. And then I remembered. My *yarmulke*. I had forgotten to put it back on.

My mother didn't say anything. She reached into her apron pocket, took out a dime and pressed it into the palm of my hand. "Here," she said. "Buy yourself some ice cream. It will cool you off."

Any other time I would've grabbed the dime and run. But this time I couldn't even think of taking her money and buying myself something with it. I held the dime out to her. "Here, Ma. I don't need it. I'll just have a glass of water or something."

"Go on, take it," she said, pushing my hand away. "Get whatever you want." She smiled at me and walked away.

I stood there staring at the dime. And then, when my mother left the room, I dropped it into the tea can.

I gulped down some cold orange juice, took a bath and went to my room to lie down. I lay there thinking about the mess I was in, and trying to figure out why I listened to Maxie in the first place. I never should have taken the money. I never should have spent a penny of what we earned.

And right then and there I decided that things

would be different from now on. I wouldn't go along with any of Maxie's ideas that didn't seem right to me. To begin with, I would go shoe shining every day until I made up that two dollars and eleven cents. I wouldn't spend a cent on anything. No eats or drinks. Nothing! If children could starve in Europe, I could starve on Surf Avenue.

My father came into my room right before supper and sat down on my bed. "Are you all right, Ari?"

"I'm fine," I said. "Just a little tired. That's all."

"You look worried. Are you sure there's nothing wrong?"

"I'm sure, Pa. I guess it's just the heat. I'll feel better when it cools off."

After supper I went up to the roof. This time I brought the watermelon. My mother cuts the slices thin. But she gives more. Maxie wasn't on the roof yet, so I started on the watermelon and practiced spitting the seeds off the roof. I was improving, not nearly as good as Maxie, but a lot better than the last time.

The steel door opened and Maxie stepped onto the roof. "Save some for me."

"I'm saving."

He picked up a piece, and right away he started spitting the seeds into the yard. "I've been planting watermelon seeds for two years now. You'd think something would be growing by this time."

"I don't think watermelon can grow in Brooklyn," I said.

We finished eating and sat down on the roof. "Boy,

Maxie. We're sure making some fortune shining shoes. According to you, we should've had twenty dollars by now, and we don't have a cent. What am I going to do? I just have to put that money back before my ma finds out."

"Tomorrow, Ari. Tomorrow for sure. We won't fool around."

A cool breeze blew in from the ocean, and there was a kind of peaceful feeling up there on the roof. Just me and Maxie and Benjy's pigeons.

"Just look at those pigeons," Maxie said. "All cooped up like that. I sure wish Benjy would let them go free. It was really funny the way he caught them. He left a trail of bread crumbs that led into the coop. And when those two pigeons walked in—slam. But I kept telling him, 'Let them go, Benjy, let them go. Birds aren't meant to be cooped up like that. They're meant to be free.' He didn't even bother to listen to me. So I don't tell him anymore."

Maxie stretched himself out on the roof with his arms folded under his head, and he looked up at the sky. "If I were a pigeon, I'd be out there flying around somewhere. I'd fly away and never come back. Wouldn't you like that, Ari? Being some kind of bird and being free?"

"Well, I'd like to fly around all right, to see what it's like up there. But then I'd want to come back home."

"Not me. I'd just keep on flying. On and on. And I'd never come back."

"Since it's pretty certain you're not going to grow

up to be a bird, what do you plan on doing? You know, when you're older."

"Oh, something exciting. Join the FBI maybe. What about you?"

"I haven't decided yet."

"Say, Ari. Let's be FBI men together. How about it?"

"Sure . . . maybe. . . ." I didn't know what to say. It's not easy telling an FBI man you want to be a cantor.

Benjy came running onto the roof. "Maxie, Mama wants you. And is she ever mad!"

Maxie slapped his forehead. "Oh no. Don't tell me Mrs. Silverman lost another pair of bloomers. Did you make any more parachutes, Benjy?"

"No, Maxie. Just that first one."

"How about it, Ari? You coming with me again?" Maxie asked.

"What for? Your mother wasn't so bad the last time."

"That's because you were there. How about it? Will you come with me this time too?"

"Sure," I said, as I got up from the floor. "I've got nothing else to do anyway." We went down the steps, with Benjy leading the way.

"Do you have any idea what's wrong?" Maxie asked him.

"Something about marbles."

Poor Maxie, I thought. First it's bloomers, then it's marbles.

When we reached Maxie's apartment, Mrs. Friedman was standing in the doorway. Holy Moses! I almost fell over. She was standing there with the shoe shine box in her hands.

"Maxie, what *is* this?"

"A . . . shoe shine box, Ma."

"I know it's a shoe shine box. I'm not blind. What are you doing with a shoe shine box?"

"Shining shoes, Ma."

"You mean to tell me you were shining shoes behind my back? You didn't even ask me?"

"I knew you'd say no."

"You're a mind reader?"

"You mean you wouldn't say no?"

"Of course I would say no. What else would I say? I ask you, Maxie. Is this a job for a Jewish boy? Is this what I send you to school for? To grow up and shine shoes?" She shrugged her shoulders and shook her head. "I don't know what to do with you, Maxie. Boardwalks, bloomers, shoe boxes . . ."

"Not the bloomers, Ma. I never took the bloomers." He looked at Benjy, and Benjy let out a little giggle.

"Tell me about the shoe shine box," Mrs. Friedman said. "I want to know why you were shining shoes."

By this time Maxie's father had come to the door. He wore an undershirt and baggy pants, and he was chewing on a spitty cigar. "Why don't you leave the boy alone?" he said. "There's nothing wrong with shining shoes. It's good honest work."

"It's a shame for the neighbors," Mrs. Friedman said.

Maxie's father shook his head. "The neighbors. Always the neighbors. That's all I ever hear from you. Listen. If you're so worried about the neighbors, why are you yelling at the boy out here, where everybody can hear? Enjoy yourself. Take him inside, close the door and you can yell at him all you want." After he said that, he turned around and walked away.

Mrs. Friedman shooed us inside and closed the door. Then she picked up right where she had left off—telling Maxie what a good-for-nothing bum he was, and how God was with her because he made Maxie's marbles roll off the dresser while she was dusting, so they would roll under the bed and lead her to the box. She went on and on. Like a nut. All I could think of was how thankful I was that I didn't have her for a mother. Maxie could keep her. Thick watermelon, fat salami and all.

After she finished with Maxie, she looked at me. "Tell me, Ari. Do you have a shoe shine box under *your* bed?"

I didn't say anything.

"You don't have to say anything, Ari. I can tell you the answer. The answer is you don't have a box under your bed. And do you know why you don't have a box under your bed? Because you respect your mother."

I turned and walked out the door.

10

Darn those marbles! Why did they have to roll under the bed? The shoe shine box was my only hope. Darn that box too.

Sooner or later my mother would be counting her money. I lived in fear of that moment. How could I look her in the eye? What would I say? I kept searching my mind for answers.

"Why so glum?" Maxie asked one afternoon when the five of us were walking home from the boardwalk. It was a few days after Mrs. Friedman made her discovery.

"You know why," I said.

"Oh that. I should've guessed." He put his hand on top of my head and gave me a couple of pats. "Ari old pal, you need to put a little fun in your life. You ought to do something to take your mind off your troubles."

"Like what?" I asked.

"Well, a good game of catch is always fun." He grabbed my *yarmulke*, called out to Brownie and threw it to him.

"Hey, cut it out!" I yelled.

Brownie threw the *yarmulke* to Lippy, who threw it to Buddy, who threw it back to Brownie.

"Okay you guys," I said. "You had your fun. Now let's have it back."

"Beanie, beanie, over here," Maxie yelled. And before I knew it, they were all running up ahead and passing my *yarmulke* back and forth like a football. Maybe they expected me to chase after them, but I didn't. I just took my time walking, acting like I didn't care what they were doing. But I did care. Because it meant that I wasn't really one of them yet. After all this time I still didn't belong.

Just as I reached 2–4, I spotted the '41 Mercury parked in front of the building. Aunt Marilyn. I called out to the others, "I'll take my *yarmulke* now. I've got to go in."

"He wants his beanie," Maxie said. "Anybody see a beanie around here?"

"Not me," Brownie said.

"Not me," Buddy said.

"Me neither," Lippy said.

"Well, forget it then," I said. "You guys can keep it." And I ran into the building.

The idea struck me as soon as I saw the car. Aunt Marilyn was almost rich. She never had to worry about subway fare or paying rent. And I bet she never went scrounging through the garbage cans for empty soda bottles.

What if I asked her for the two dollars and eleven cents? It could be an advance on my Chanukah money. Every December, for the holiday of Chanukah, she gives me two or three silver dollars. Maybe I could get it now. Today. An early Chanukah. The idea was growing as I ran up the stairs. I could hear my mother talking in the kitchen when I opened the door.

"Every morning I go down to the mailbox and look for Etta's letter. But nothing ever comes."

"Sarah, the war can't last much longer. When it's all over, you'll hear from her, I'm sure."

"That's why it's so important for me to go to Chicago to see Leah. Who knows? Maybe she's all I have left."

"Listen, Sarah, you don't have to save your pennies like that. I'll give you the money. Pay me back whenever you can."

That sure did sound like Aunt Marilyn all right— offering money like that. She knows my mother wouldn't take a dime from her. Sometimes I think she just comes over to gloat.

"Thank you, no," my mother said. "I have almost enough now."

"It isn't right that you should have to count every cent like that. Even if he is my brother, I have to say it. Abe isn't doing a very good job of providing for you."

"He works hard, Malkeh. Very hard. He does his best."

I would have gone into the kitchen, but I waited in the foyer so I could listen.

"After all," Aunt Marilyn continued, "you'd think that a man who works in a mink shop should at least be able to bring his wife home a little mink coat once in a while."

"Ah, Malkeh, Malkeh. Of all the things in this world, what I need most is a mink coat. A mink coat to wear when I go to the delicatessen or sit on a bench in the park or go for my walks around the block. I can't understand you. With all the suffering in Europe, with that maniac Hitler, how can you think of mink coats?"

When I heard my mother's voice cracking, I knew it was time to make my entrance. "Hi, everyone."

"Lionel darling."

"Ari. I didn't hear you come in."

"My sneakers are very quiet," I said.

Aunt Marilyn came over and put her arms around me. "So how do you like your new neighborhood, Lionel darling?"

"Well, it sure is different than Rivington was. The guys are a lot different too."

She ran her fingers through my hair and seemed pleased to find that my head was bare. "I see you don't wear your *yarmulke* anymore."

"Yes, I still wear it. I just lost it, that's all."

"Oh," she said, and sniffed. Then she took a deep breath and went on talking. "I worry about you, Lionel. Having to make all new friends, people who are different from the kind you're used to, having to adjust to a new school in September." She gave my head a little pat and smiled. "Well, dear, at least you'll be going to a public school and not to that parochial school, whatever it's called."

"The Rabbi Jacob Joseph Yeshiva," I told her.

"How was I to know that the yeshiva here only goes to the fourth grade?" my mother said. "So it looks like we'll have to wait until he's old enough to travel on the subway, and then he can go back to the yeshiva."

"In the meantime I'll go to public school and to Hebrew School afterward," I said.

Aunt Marilyn shot up from her chair. "Hebrew School? Sarah, the boy's had enough already. He doesn't need any more Hebrew. He should be out in the fresh air. Not shut up in a musty, old building somewhere."

"The building isn't musty, Aunt Marilyn. And I get plenty of fresh air."

"See, Malkeh. The building isn't musty. And he gets plenty of fresh air."

"He should be out playing."

"I get enough playing."

"Malkeh, there's more to life than playing."

I got tired of defending myself, so I just shut up and let my mother do all the defending for me. But I waited around for a chance to ask Aunt Marilyn for the money.

"Look at him, Malkeh," my mother was saying. "Did I do such a bad job with my son? You remember how you told me I shouldn't speak Yiddish to him? That he'll grow up to be a greenhorn, a *mockey*? Tell me, Malkeh, does he look like a *mockey* to you?"

"Well, I have to admit, you had me worried for a while. After all, a three-year-old American boy speaking Yiddish all the time. Not knowing a word of English. What was I to think?"

My mother was beaming all over the place. "So now he knows not only one language but two. And soon he'll be speaking a perfect Hebrew. And that will make three."

"But Sarah, I still don't understand what he needs Hebrew School for, what he needs a *yarmulke* for. It's good he lost it. Let it stay lost."

What was going on, I wondered. Why was my *yarmulke* so important to everyone all of a sudden? It's always been a natural part of my clothing.

"Speak up, Lionel dear. Did you want to say something?"

"No, Aunt Marilyn. I didn't want to say anything."

"Good. Because I still have plenty to say. I want to say that we are living in America, and America is The Melting Pot, and in America you have to melt."

"Melt, shmelt," my mother said.

"Sarah, you simply refuse to learn—to better yourself. I talk about The Melting Pot, and you make jokes."

"What jokes? Listen, Malkeh, if melting means I have to forget where I come from and who I am and what I believe, then no thank you. I don't want to melt."

"Sarah, what am I going to do with you? The whole idea of America is The Melting Pot. Don't you see that? We all have to become like one. The same. Can't I make you understand anything?"

"But why, Aunt Marilyn?" I asked. "Why does everyone have to be like everyone else?"

"Lionel, don't interrupt me. I have to make your mother understand."

"But Aunt Marilyn, maybe you're the one who doesn't understand."

When I said that, she turned red in the face. "*I* don't understand? *I* don't understand? Listen to him. My educated nephew in the sixth grade. My dear Lionel, don't tell me I don't understand. I understand plenty. I'm a little older than you, you know. I've lived a little longer than you, you know. Don't talk to me about understanding."

"But Aunt Marilyn. I'm old enough to know what The Melting Pot means. And it means just the opposite of what you say. It doesn't mean that everyone should become like everyone else. It means that all kinds of people from all kinds of backgrounds can come and live together and contribute something of themselves. We're already part of The Melting Pot."

My mother smiled at me and said, "See, Malkeh. He goes to a yeshiva, and still he knows about The Melting Pot."

"But Sarah, Hebrew School? Hebrew? What does he need it for? It's a dead language. When will he or anyone else ever speak Hebrew?"

"Someday, Malkeh. Someday when the Jews return

90

to Palestine. Everyone there will be speaking Hebrew."

"Jews have been dreaming of a return to Palestine for two thousand years. Do you really believe you'll see it in your lifetime? Palestine is a dream, Sarah. Just a dream. And you . . . you're nothing but a dreamer."

"Sometimes all we have are our dreams," my mother said. "And sometimes dreams come true." Her voice started to crack again. "Palestine. If we had Palestine today, Etta and her family would have a place to go . . . instead of . . ."

I looked up at my mother's face and saw her eyes brimming. This time Aunt Marilyn had gone too far. And she wouldn't let up. "Now Sarah," she began. But I wouldn't let her finish.

"Leave her alone," I yelled at her. "Will you please just leave her alone?" And right then and there I knew I would never ask Aunt Marilyn for the money. I would never ask her for anything.

11

I didn't go to the synagogue that Saturday, or the Saturday after that, or any Saturday in the whole month of August. It had nothing to do with wanting to sleep late. It's just that I couldn't bring myself to go to services until I got every cent of my mother's money back in her *pushke*. I just couldn't see myself walking into a synagogue like I was some kind of holy person or something, sitting around all those holy books and maybe singing *"Adon Olam"* and having everyone congratulate me like they did the last time. Maybe I was a thief and a liar, but I wasn't a hypocrite.

My mother and father were very upset, especially my mother. "Ari, it's *Shabbos*. Come to *shul*."

"Not this week, Ma, please. Maybe next week."

"You say that every *Shabbos*. It's always next week."

And my father. "Ari, if you could tell me what's wrong . . ."

"There's nothing wrong, Pa. I just don't feel like going."

My father put a hand on top of my head. "Ari, in all the years past, ever since you were old enough to walk,

92

you hardly ever missed going to *shul* with me on *Shabbos*. What's happened?"

"I'm not sure, exactly. I don't really know. I guess it's just that going to *shul* was a lot easier then. All the kids I knew used to go, and here nobody goes. And all kinds of things have been happening. Everything's different. Nothing's the same anymore."

My father cupped my face in his hands and lifted it so he could look into my eyes. "You're the same, aren't you?" I shrugged my shoulders and thought, You should only know.

Sometimes at night, whenever my mother and father thought I was asleep, I could hear the two of them whispering in the kitchen. "Abe, we made a mistake. We never should have moved here. There are so many beautiful neighborhoods in Brooklyn. So many beautiful streets where boys like Ari live. Why did we have to pick Nass Walk? The boys here are a bad influence on him. A bunch of bums. I'm worried that he'll become a bum too."

"We have to have faith in him, Sarah. Faith that he'll choose the right way. We'll have to wait and see what happens. We have to give him time."

"Time? It's just getting worse. What we tried to do for him in a lifetime—poof! In two months of Nass Walk—finished!"

"If two months of Nass Walk can undo everything we did, then we didn't do anything."

But Maxie was proud of me. He congratulated me

every time I stayed home from the synagogue. To him, not going there meant that I was well on my way to becoming an All-American Boy. Maxie and the others thought I was more All-American for another reason. I stopped wearing my *yarmulke* when I was with them. I wanted to wear it. I felt naked with my head bare. But I got sick and tired of having them make such a fuss over it all the time. It was easier to take my *yarmulke* off and put it in my pocket before I went out.

As for Saturdays, it never seemed like we ever did anything that was so All-American. Mostly we just sat around, trying to decide what to do or where to go. But everything anybody suggested, like going to a ball game or a movie, cost too much money.

A few times we went under the boardwalk and peeked up through the cracks. I was still the only one who couldn't see anything.

By the end of August I was beginning to wonder if I'd ever see the inside of a synagogue again. If I was waiting for that two dollars and eleven cents, I probably wouldn't. That money was nowhere in sight.

One night after supper we were sitting around the table, drinking our tea out of glasses. I was working on my P-38. I had all the parts sanded and glued together, and all I had left was the painting.

My mother was in the middle of one of her favorite subjects—how time flies. She likes to say things like, "It seems only yesterday that Ari was born, and soon

he'll have his *Bar Mitzvah*." Or, "It seems like yesterday when I came to this country. Where do the years
go?"

"Abe," she was saying, "where does the time go? It
seems like yesterday that we moved from Rivington
Street, and here it is, almost Rosh Hashanah. Last year
we celebrated the holidays on the East Side. This year
in Brooklyn. And next year—who knows?"

My mother walked over to the window sill and
picked up the tea can.

"I should have enough by now," she said. "God willing, I'll see Leah by Chanukah." She brought the can
to the table and sat down. When she lifted the lid, I
knew she meant business, and I froze. What I needed
that very second was two dollars and eleven cents or a
miracle. It was easy to see that I wasn't going to get the
two dollars and eleven cents. So I prayed for the miracle and looked at my mother. My father looked at
me.

"Sarah," he said, "why not wait a few weeks to count
the money, after Rosh Hashanah and Yom Kippur. To
mark the beginning of a year. Not the end."

"Maybe so, Abe. Maybe so." She closed the lid and
put the tea can back on the window sill.

Ah, my father, my miracle.

After my mother cleared the table, she went into the
living room to read this book Mrs. Silverman had lent
her, *A Tree Grows in Brooklyn*. Mrs. Silverman told her
she would have a good cry over it, and there's nothing

95

my mother likes better than a good cry over a book.

My father and I were left alone. He sat there, looking at me. I swallowed the lump in my throat. "You know, don't you?" I asked.

"Yes, from the very beginning. I came back that night to keep you company, and I saw you with the money."

"The noise at the door . . . it was you. But why didn't you tell me you knew? All this time and you didn't say a thing to me."

"I was hoping you would tell me about it yourself."

"I wasn't really stealing the money, Pa. Honest."

"I know, Ari."

"I was just going to use it to make more money—not only for me but for Ma too. For her hat and her trip to Chicago. It was supposed to be a surprise. Boy, some surprise." And I told my father the whole story, starting with Jack's fortune and ending with the marbles rolling under Maxie's bed.

"Maybe I can give you the money," my father said. "I have a little extra this week."

"Thanks, Pa, but I'd feel just as bad taking the money from you. I have to get it myself, somehow."

"Why don't you tell Mama what happened? I'm sure she'll understand that you meant well."

"I can't, Pa. I just can't. She'll get that look on her face. I hate to see her looking that way. And I know how disappointed she's been in me lately. I don't want to disappoint her anymore."

"She's not disappointed in you, Ari. She's just confused. And frankly, so am I. You stopped going to *shul*; you don't wear your *yarmulke* as much as you used to. Have these things lost all meaning for you?"

"They're still important to me, Pa. But sometimes they get in the way."

"I don't understand. They get in the way of what?"

"I don't know how to explain it, exactly. But I've made all these new friends here, and certain things make it harder for me to be part of them."

"Ah, yes," my father said. "I think I understand now. But may I ask you, how much are you willing to give up to be part of them?"

"I don't want to give up anything. But I don't want to be different from them either. It isn't easy being different."

"It never is. It never has been. Take the Sunday Blue Laws, for example. It would be easier for me to work on Saturday instead of having to pay fines or going to court to try and fight them. But why should I give up my beliefs and what I hold sacred just to be like other people want me to be?

"I was different when I came to this country from Russia and was looked upon by some people as an ignorant greenhorn, because I couldn't speak English."

"That's crazy," I said. "You couldn't speak English, but you could speak Russian and Hebrew and Yiddish. And you could read and write in all three languages too."

"That didn't seem to matter to those people. They only saw what they wanted to see—that I was different from them. Even now, because I speak English with an accent, I'm still an ignorant greenhorn."

"It's not fair that people think you're ignorant when you know even more than they do," I said.

"Ari, you can't help what people think. The important thing is for you yourself to know what you are . . . and who you are."

My father stood up and walked around the room for a while. Then he turned to me and said, "Ari, whenever you begin to worry about being different and try so hard to be like everyone else, I'd like you to think of that saying of Hillel's, 'If I am not for myself, who will be for me?' You asked me about it once, and I told you it means more than it says. It means more than liking yourself or caring about yourself. It means that *you* are the one who will determine the kind of person you will be. No one can determine that for you. Of all the choices to be made in life, the final choice is yours."

While I was thinking about Hillel, I heard a knock on the door. I opened it, and there was Maxie with this huge burlap sack.

"Hi, Maxie," I said. "What's in the sack?"

"Just you wait and see."

I helped him drag the sack to my room, and he untied it. "It looks like confetti," I said.

"It is confetti. My pop got it from a guy he works

with. He sells confetti on the side—for parades and things."

"Great. Now all we need is a parade."

"We've got one," Maxie said. "The Mardi Gras. Every year at the end of summer there's a whole week's celebration on Surf Avenue. Every night, parades, confetti . . . it's wild."

"It's an awful lot of confetti for just the two of us to throw around," I said.

"We're not going to throw it. We're going to sell it."

I practically threw him out of my room. "Oh no! Count me out. I'm not getting mixed up in any more of your . . ."

"Don't get so excited," Maxie interrupted. "I'm only doing this for your own good. I could ask any of the guys to sell this with me, and they'd jump at the chance. But I know how much you need the money. So will you at least listen to me?"

"Okay, I'm listening."

"The whole thing's simple. And you don't have to invest a cent. All we do is get a bunch of little bags and fill them up with this confetti. When the Mardi Gras starts, we take them down to Surf Avenue and sell them. Three bags for a dime. They were selling confetti last year. Everybody was buying it. We'll make a million dollars. I guarantee it. And we don't have to do it secretly. There's nothing wrong with Jewish boys selling confetti. I checked with my ma."

"It sounds okay so far, but where do we get all those little bags?"

"We can buy them at the grocery or someplace. My pop already loaned me some money. He wouldn't give me the money if he didn't think we could sell the stuff, would he?"

"I guess not."

"Well then, do you want to do it or don't you?"

"I'll do it, Maxie. I sure need that money."

The next morning we went around to all the stores in the neighborhood to buy bags. I dug up a batch of small ones from behind our refrigerator, where my mother keeps all her spare bags, and we sent Benjy around to collect some from the neighbors at 2–4.

"If anybody can get bags from those old ladies, Benjy can," Maxie said. "They can't resist him."

By the afternoon we had about two hundred small bags. We spent the rest of the day in the alley, filling them up with confetti and piling them up in small cardboard boxes. We fixed the boxes up with string so we could carry them around our necks. On the boxes in black crayon we wrote:

CONFETTI
3 BAGS
10¢

Altogether we had five boxes. Two for Maxie, two for me and one for Benjy.

On the first evening of the Mardi Gras we wore our boxes over to Surf Avenue. A large crowd was gathering along the street, and we started selling the confetti right away. We walked up and down Surf Avenue. The best spot was right in front of Nathan's. That place is always packed.

Sometimes I'd yell, "Confetti, three for a dime!" Or, "Get your confetti before it's too late!" But mostly I didn't even have to open my mouth. People just came up and handed me the money and grabbed the bags themselves.

Lots of cops were out there too, to keep everything orderly, I guess. One of them started walking toward me, and I thought, This is it! I'm selling confetti without a license, and I'm only eleven.

The cop came closer and I froze to the spot. I tried to figure out what Maxie would do in a situation like this. So when he came up to me, I looked him straight in the eye and forced a smile. "Hi, Officer. Would you like a bag of confetti?"

He smiled back. "No thanks, kid." And he just walked away.

In the distance I could hear the parade starting up. And that's when the confetti really started to sell. I got rid of the batch I had and ran home to get my second box.

When I got back, the parade was in full swing. The crowds were so thick, I could hardly get through them. Little kids were sitting on top of their fathers' shoul-

ders, waving balloons and throwing confetti at the marching bands and floats that passed by. There were policemen on horseback and clowns and baton twirlers in skimpy costumes. There was so much celebrating, you'd think the war was over instead of just the summer.

In no time at all I was sold out of confetti, and the parade was still going strong. With an empty box, a pocketful of money, and the sounds of the drums and bugles ringing in my ears, I left Surf Avenue and ran home. I couldn't believe it! After all those weeks of empty pockets, I now had money to jingle.

When I got there, Maxie and Benjy were already on the roof, counting their money. As soon as Maxie saw me, he came running over and started laughing and punching me.

"Didn't I tell you we'd make a million? Didn't I tell you? And we could've made ten times as much if we would've had more confetti."

"I bet I've got a hundred dollars right here," Benjy said, looking up from his pile of money.

When we counted our enormous fortune, we found that we didn't quite make a million. It was more like six dollars and sixty-eight cents. We took out the money for the tea can and the money Maxie owed his father for the bags, and we split the rest according to the number of bags we each sold. Maxie and I each ended up with a dollar seventy-five, and we gave Benjy fifty cents. Not bad for a seven-year-old kid.

"What are you going to do with all that money?" I asked Benjy.

"I'm putting it in my bank," he said.

"Yeah," Maxie said. "This kid's got a bank stashed away someplace, and he won't even tell me where it is."

"That's good thinking, Benjy," I said.

"Hey Ari," Maxie said. "A thought just popped into my head. Why don't we go out and use this money to buy a few more sacks of confetti? We still have a whole week left of the Mardi Gras and . . ."

I didn't wait for him to finish. "Good night, Maxie," I said. And I got off that roof fast.

I went back to my apartment. My mother and father were still outside, talking to the neighbors. I went into the kitchen, walked over to the tea can and lifted the lid. I reached into my pocket and took out the two dollars and eleven cents and put it back into the can. Then I reached into my other pocket and took out another dollar's worth of change and put that in too.

"Well, Ma," I whispered, "I can't send you to Chicago or buy you all those new hats for the holidays, but at least I can treat you to your feather."

That night, for the first time since I took the money, sleep came fast and easy. And I had a dream. A strange dream. Moses was looking down at me from the top of Mount Sinai. And he was smiling.

12

With seventy-five cents in my pocket I felt like a millionaire. The only trouble was, now that I had some money, there was no place and no time to spend it. Our summer vacation had come to an end.

My mother decided that it was about time I got myself a haircut. She figured if I got the haircut at the beginning of September, I'd look real neat for school and still be presentable when the Jewish holidays would start on the seventeenth.

I got the haircut and was all set for my first day at PS 100. I was so nervous about entering a new school, especially a public school, that I kept going to the bathroom all morning. And when my mother made me eat a whole bowlful of farina and wished me good luck, I felt a whole lot worse.

As usual, I had taken my *yarmulke* off before I left the building and put it in my pocket. I didn't want Maxie or Brownie to knock it off my head and start another game of football with it. I would've had to take it off anyway, because boys aren't allowed to wear *yarmulke*s in public school. In my other school you couldn't get in without one.

I walked to school with the rest of the guys. They looked so clean, you could hardly recognize anybody, except for Buddy, of course, who was his usual neat self. We all wore new shirts and pants and regular shoes instead of sneakers.

I don't think I would've been so afraid to go to school if Maxie was in my class. But he and Buddy were in seventh grade and I was in sixth. I hoped I would at least be in the same room with Lippy and Brownie. They were in sixth grade too. Actually, Brownie belonged in seventh, but he was behind because he flunked first grade.

PS 100 is on West Third Street right next to the synagogue. Hundreds of kids were swarming around the building. Hundreds of them, and I knew four.

"If you survive the first day, it won't be so bad," Maxie assured me. "I know. I went through all this when I moved here from Brownsville."

It turned out that I was in the same room with Brownie and Lippy. It was better than nothing. The classroom was a strange sight. Bareheaded boys, and lots of girls too. At my other school all we had were boys.

Right away Brownie ran to the back of the room and grabbed a seat in the last row. Lippy, of course, ran after him. I plunked myself down in the middle of the room, so I wouldn't be too conspicuous in either direction.

This kid Sheldon Greenspan sat across the aisle from

me. He had shaggy brown hair that looked like it was growing into his eyes. I knew what his name was because he had it written all over his notebook:

SHELDON GREENSPAN
SHELDON GREENSPAN
SHELDON GREENSPAN

Pretty soon the teacher walked in. She was a tall lady, and her hair, which was part black and part gray, was wrapped in a bun at the nape of her neck, just like my mother wears her hair when she gets all dressed up. She wrote her name on the board:

MRS. LASKER

Then she turned around and said, "Hello, my name is Mrs. Lasker. Welcome to Room 210, sixth grade. You may sit anyplace you'd like, as long as you behave."

She took attendance, and we spent the first part of the morning passing out books. Then we had recess. When we came back, Mrs. Lasker caught Brownie giving Lippy a piggyback ride in the room, so she moved them both up to the front where she could keep an eye on them.

Mrs. Lasker said she wanted to begin the new school year by having us stand up and introduce ourselves and tell what we did during the summer.

Some of the kids said they couldn't remember what they did, and others said they didn't do anything. Sheldon Greenspan said he visited his grandmother in New Jersey. All the events of the summer started to flash through my mind—hiding under the boardwalk, sneaking into Luna Park, shining shoes, selling confetti. . . . I had a hard time deciding what I could talk about.

When Mrs. Lasker called on Brownie, he stood up next to his seat and said, "My name is Brownie and I went to the beach."

Then it was Lippy's turn. "My name is Lippy and I went to the beach with Brownie."

She finally called on me. "My name is Ari and I went to the beach with Brownie and Lippy." And by that time, the morning was over.

The five of us walked home together at lunchtime and then again after school.

"Let's take a walk on Brighton and figure out a way to spend all our money," Maxie said to me.

"I can't. I've got Hebrew School at four. I'll have just enough time to grab a bite to eat and fool around for a little while before I go."

"Aw, come on, Ari. What do you need that Hebrew for anyway? It'll turn you into a real *mockey*."

"Boy, you sound just like my aunt," I said. "But today is the first day of class, so I'd better go."

"Me too," Brownie said. "I'll go with you. Misery loves company."

"Hey Brownie," I said. "I didn't know you went to Hebrew too."

"Yeah, my ma makes me."

Maxie started to laugh. "Brownie is some student. Hebrew runs from Monday through Thursday, and he manages to go about once a week."

Then Lippy said, "Maybe you can ditch tomorrow, huh, Brownie?"

"Sure. After today I'm through for the week."

The Hebrew School is located in the synagogue on West Third Street. When Brownie and I walked over there at four, he said, "Only one more year of this stuff. When I'm thirteen, I can quit."

"You don't like it much, do you?" I asked.

He shook his head. "I don't like anything that has to do with school." He paused for a moment, and then he looked straight at me. "It's hard to like somethin' you're not good in."

"Well, I'm sure glad you're with me today, Brownie. I feel a lot better with you around. I hate walking into strange places alone."

He smiled. "Yeah? Well, don't worry about a thing. You just follow me."

We found the right room in just a few minutes. Brownie was in the class with me. He flunked first grade in Hebrew too.

Some of the kids from my class at PS 100 were there. Sheldon Greenspan was one of them. Only it turned out that in Hebrew School they called him Shepsy. He looked more like a Shepsy than a Sheldon, so from then on I called him Shepsy too.

The teacher, Mr. Kolodny, was a short middle-aged

man with glasses. He greeted us at the door with a smile and a *Shalom*. Then he took attendance and welcomed everyone to the class. After that he did what Mrs. Lasker did. He asked each one of us to stand up and introduce ourselves and tell what we did during the summer. Only we had to tell it in Hebrew. I guess he was trying to be real modern.

While Shepsy told about his grandmother in New Jersey, I saw a look of panic on Brownie's face. So on a piece of paper I wrote down the Hebrew translation for *I went to the sea*, and slipped it to Brownie. I hoped he knew how to read. You can't learn much by going one day a week.

Brownie smiled at me when he saw the paper, and he started to study it right away. When it was his turn, he stood up and recited the words.

"*Tov m'od*, very good," Mr. Kolodny said. And the widest grin I'd ever seen in my life spread across Brownie's face.

When I was called on, I told how I went to the beach with Brownie because we were friends.

"You know somethin'?" Brownie said on the way home. "It wasn't so bad today. Maybe I'll go with you again tomorrow."

I took advantage of Brownie's moment of weakness and said, "We sure did talk a lot about the beach today. And I was wondering something, Brownie. Can you really see much when you're under the boardwalk? Because I can't see anything."

110

"Mostly I see feet," he said. "I could see more if sand didn't get in my eyes all the time."

"Thanks, Brownie," I said. "That's all I wanted to know."

13

A few days before the High Holidays, my mother went out shopping for her new feather.

"See, I put it on already," she said, showing us the new red feather sewed onto her old black hat. "All I did was give the hat a little brushing and put the feather on. It's almost like new."

On Monday and Tuesday my mother wore her almost-like-new hat to the synagogue for Rosh Hashanah. Rosh Hashanah is a very important holiday. Not only does it mark the beginning of the Jewish New Year and the creation of the world, but it's a time for people to look deep inside themselves and try to judge their thoughts and actions of the past year, at the same time pledging to do better in the year ahead. Not only does the year take on a new beginning, people can begin again too.

I knew that I needed to take a deep look inside myself, so I went with my mother and father to the synagogue. The streets were filled with men, women and kids walking to services. And a large crowd of people were milling around in front of the synagogue, wishing each other, *"Shanah tovah tikasevu"*—May you be inscribed (in *The Book of Life*) to have a good year.

I remember thinking, when I went inside, that there sure were a lot of people who had come to look inside themselves. Most of the benches were filled. My father and I finally found a couple of empty spaces in the back. My mother went upstairs to the balcony to sit in the women's section.

Maxie, Lippy, Brownie and Brownie's older brother, Jack, stayed out of school because of the holidays. They got all dressed up in their blue suits and went to the synagogue for about ten minutes. When Jack's mother and father were safely seated, Jack sneaked out to the alley to work on the '32 Ford he bought. Maxie, Brownie and Lippy went with him.

Buddy stayed home from school too. He said that ever since his first year at PS 100, when he was the only kid who came to class on Rosh Hashanah, he started taking off on the Jewish holidays too.

The services were led by a cantor called in especially for the holidays. He stood there in his white robe, his blue-and-white prayer shawl covering his head, swaying his body backward and forward and singing softly. A humming and chanting filled the synagogue, and pretty soon I was so caught up in the sweetness of his voice and the beauty of the Hebrew melodies that I knew for sure I would someday become a cantor. It had been so long since I'd been to services, I'd almost forgotten how good they made me feel. Maybe I wasn't so All-American after all.

When it came time for the blowing of the *shofar*, the ram's horn, all the little kids who were outside came running in to listen. When I turned around to look at them, I saw Maxie, Brownie, Lippy and Buddy standing in the doorway. Then above the hush came the sounding of the *shofar*. And that made it official. It was the Jewish New Year, 5705.

On the second day of the holiday, just before sunset, Maxie and I went up to the roof to watch the night come to Brooklyn. Brooklyn is always so vast in the daytime, but on a quiet summer's night it's just that tiny spot of roof on 2–4 Nass Walk. And when we're up there, it's like we're the only two people left in the whole world.

That evening though, there was one other person left in the world. We found him crouched in a corner of the roof.

"Benjy?" Maxie called softly. "You all right?"

Benjy turned toward us, tears spilling out of his eyes, a grayish blob cupped in his hands. "Look," he cried. "There's something wrong with my pigeon. He's not moving."

We looked at the still form he was holding. Maxie shook his head. "Sorry, Benjy. But your pigeon's dead. That's what's wrong with him."

"But he can't be dead," Benjy cried. "His eyes are open and he's looking at me. How can he be dead if he's looking at me?"

"He can't see you. He can't see anything anymore."

"It's all my fault," Benjy sobbed. "If I would've let him go free like you told me, he wouldn't be dead now. It's all my fault."

"It's not your fault, Benjy," I said. "It would've happened anyway. Pigeons get old and sick—just like people."

"Sure," Maxie said. "Don't cry. You still have your other one. And if you want, I'll catch you a brand-new pigeon tomorrow."

"I don't want a brand-new pigeon!" Benjy screamed. "I want this one."

"Listen, Benjy," I said. "I've got an idea. We'll have a funeral for your pigeon. Right now. We'll bury him in the backyard, where he'll always be close to you. Would you like that?"

Benjy nodded and still clutching the pigeon, wiped his eyes on his arms.

"I'll go get a box," I said, "and meet you two down in the yard." I went to my room and found a shoe box in the closet. By the time I came down with it, Maxie was already digging the little grave.

It was dark now, except for the light from a nearby street lamp that filtered through the trees, casting shadows on the ground. Maxie finished digging, and Benjy gently placed the pigeon inside the shoe box.

"Do you think we need a rabbi?" Benjy asked me.

"I think we can handle this one ourselves," I said. "But if you want, we can say something in Hebrew. Something short and simple."

"Like *shalom*?"

"Yes, Benjy. Like *shalom*. That's perfect."

"Will that be the *shalom* that means good-bye or the *shalom* that means peace?" Maxie asked.

"Both," Benjy said quickly. "I want it to mean both. Good-bye *and* peace."

"Then it'll mean both," I said, and I placed the box in the ground. Maxie and Benjy took turns throwing handfuls of earth on top of it.

When the box was all covered, Benjy let out a deep sigh. "I guess he's gone now," he said. "I don't have him anymore."

"You'll have him in your memory," I said. "As long as you don't forget him, he won't really be gone."

"Oh, I won't ever forget him," he said. "Not ever."

He sifted some more dirt over the grave and flattened the ground on top of it. Maxie put his arm around his brother's shoulder. "I guess it's time to say it now, Benjy."

"Yeah. I guess."

We huddled together in the shadows of the trees.

"*Shalom*, pigeon," Benjy whispered.

14

Yom Kippur, the most important Jewish holiday of all, came the following Wednesday. It's a day that's supposed to be spent in the synagogue asking God to forgive all your sins of the past year. Sins against Him and sins against other people.

God will forgive our sins against Him. But he will only forgive our sins against others if we first try to make peace with them ourselves. We have to try to make it up to those we've hurt and ask their forgiveness. We have to forgive too, and sometimes that can be even harder.

I knew that if I expected forgiveness for taking the money from my mother's tea can, I'd have to go to her and tell her what I did. But I couldn't do that yet. Maybe someday but not yet.

I decided that I would go to the synagogue and sit there all day. From sunrise to sunset. And to prove how sorry I was and how much I wanted to be forgiven, I would fast for a whole day. No food or water would pass through my lips for twenty-four hours. Kids under thirteen don't have to fast on Yom Kippur, except maybe for an hour or two as they get older, to sort of get used to it. Every year I try to fast the whole day like my mother and father do. But I usually give out by about ten-thirty in the morning. For some reason I'm always hungrier and thirstier on Yom Kippur than on any other day of the year.

"I'm really going to fast this time," I told the guys on the way home from school Tuesday. "Starting this evening at sunset, all the way until tomorrow at sunset."

"You'll never make it," Brownie said.

"Sure I will. I plan on eating about one hundred of my mother's *kreplach* tonight, and that should keep me going all day tomorrow."

That evening I stuffed myself with *kreplach* and drank about two gallons of water. I could fast for a week with all that I had in my stomach. After supper, just before sunset, my mother put a few coins in the *pushkes* and lit the candles. Then we went to the synagogue to hear the cantor sing the most beautiful prayer of the whole holiday, *"Kol Nidre."*

My father and I went to services again about eight o'clock the next morning. I felt great. For me, fasting would be a snap. During the first hour I went through the services like a breeze—reading and singing in Hebrew, standing up when I was supposed to stand up and sitting down when I was supposed to sit down.

After a while all that reading and singing made my mouth and throat dry, so I limited myself to the singing and read with my eyes. When my vision started to blur, I just listened to the prayers and said the ones I knew by heart. By ten-thirty I was too weak to stand up, and my stomach felt like an empty pit. But I stuck it out till noon.

"Ari," my father said, "go home and have lunch. You shouldn't fast so long."

"I only have seven more hours to go," I managed to say in my weak voice. "I'll make it."

"You'll make yourself sick. That's what you'll do. Now go home and eat something."

"Just a little longer, Pa."

"Then go outside and get some fresh air. You look pale."

I didn't want to overdo my martyrdom, so I decided to go out and see what Maxie and the other guys were doing. Maybe they would help me take my mind off my hunger.

I walked out of the synagogue like I was in a stupor and made my way back to Nass Walk. Nobody was there, so I went into the alley behind 1–3. Maxie and the others were sitting on boxes and garbage cans, watching Jack, who had his head buried under the hood of his '32 Ford. Since you're not supposed to do any kind of work on the holidays, I figured he had probably waited for his mother and father to leave for the synagogue before he went into the alley.

The car was dented and dirty, and there were two tires missing, but it was pretty terrific-looking anyway.

"Hi, Ari," Maxie called. "How long did you hold out?"

"I'm still holding," I said, looking at Lippy, who was

at his polly seeds again. "I haven't had a thing to eat or drink since supper."

"I can believe it," Maxie said. "You don't look so good."

"How about some nice, cold, fresh water?" Brownie asked.

"No thanks. I'll be all right."

I looked at Lippy and his polly seeds again. He licked the salt off each shell before he cracked it open. He ate the seed and then made a big thing out of licking his lips. He was torturing me with each lick.

"Are you sure you don't want water?" Brownie asked again. "Just a little, tiny sip? We won't tell."

"No thanks," I said. "If you just quit talking about water, I'll be okay."

"How much longer do you have to go?" Buddy asked.

"What time is it?"

"I don't know. I don't have a watch. Does anybody here have a watch?"

"Yeah," Brownie said. "Jack's got a watch. Hey, Jack! What time is it?"

"It's 12:17 on the button," he called out from under the hood.

"It's 12:17 on the button," Brownie repeated, like I couldn't hear for myself.

I made a few quick calculations in my mind. "Only six hours and forty-three minutes to go," I said.

Buddy got up from a box and brushed his pants off.

"It's 12:17, huh? Well, I'll see you guys later. I've got to go get some lunch. I'm starved. I've got all kinds of delicious things waiting for me at home."

"I'm starved too," Maxie said. "I've been fasting since breakfast. And I didn't have much of a breakfast either. Just about fifteen wheat cakes smothered with butter and all this gooey syrup running all over." He was smacking his lips like crazy.

Lippy was doing double time with his polly seeds. I knew what these guys were trying to do.

"I bet they were fat wheat cakes," I said. "Fat like the salami and rye bread and watermelon."

"What are you talking about?" Maxie asked.

"Nothing. You wouldn't understand."

"Hey, guys," Maxie said. "Listen to Ari. He's delirious. All that thirst and hunger affected his head."

"Are you sure you don't want water?" Brownie teased.

"Yeah, Isidore. Come to think of it, that's a good idea. Go upstairs and get me some. A big potful. Just bring it down here, and I'll soak your head in it."

Then I remembered it was Yom Kippur, and you're not supposed to be mean to people. All my suffering would be for nothing. So I said, "I'm sorry, Brownie. Forget what I said about the water."

Maxie walked over to me. "Hey, Ari. I hope you're not mad. We were only poking fun. It's just that nobody believes in that stuff anymore."

"I do," I said. And I went back to the synagogue.

As soon as I sat down next to my father, I knew I wouldn't last till seven. I figured I'd probably faint away at any second.

My father looked at me. "Ari, I'm very proud of you. But enough is enough. It's a sin to endanger your health. That's why there are some people who are not even allowed to fast. The very old, the very young and the sick. That's the law."

Well, I was young all right, and I sure was sick. Two out of three. "Okay, Pa, I'll go up and see Ma for a while, and then I'll go home and eat."

I made my way upstairs to the ladies' section. There I saw all these ladies praying and crying softly into their handkerchiefs. The men cry too, I guess. But it's harder to tell. They blow their noses and act like they've got colds. The ladies cry open and unashamed. Every Yom Kippur they come to the synagogue and cry. But I never noticed it as much as I did this time. Maybe the people in Brooklyn have more sins than the people on the East Side, but I don't think so. The old ladies cry more than anyone. I guess it must be because they sit there wondering if God will let them live to see another year.

I finally found my mother, and the ladies moved over on the bench so I could sit next to her. She bent over and kissed me. And even though she smiled, I could see that faraway look in her eyes, and I could tell that she had been crying. I just know she was crying for her sister in Europe. I saw the same kind of

122

look on some of the other faces around me. I guess lots of people had sisters or someone in Europe.

So I just sat there for a while and watched all the ladies cry. Then I left the synagogue and dragged myself back to 2–4, up the three flights of stairs and into the apartment.

I headed straight for the kitchen sink, turned on the faucet and let the water pour into my mouth. I opened the refrigerator and grabbed at all the food in sight. I didn't know what, and I didn't care. All I know is, I just opened up my mouth and shoveled everything in.

15

At the beginning of October when the High Holidays were over, my mother greeted the New Year by counting the money in her tea can. She found that she had enough for train fare to Chicago. So right away she sat down and wrote a letter telling Leah that she would be there for Chanukah.

At school, Mrs. Lasker greeted the New Year by announcing that a model-airplane contest would be held in the gym sometime in November. There would be two categories—flying models and solids. I was really looking forward to it. I had my P-38 solid all finished, so I was all set.

Maxie already had the plane I had given him, and Buddy and Lippy each bought a B-17 solid. Brownie was going to buy one too, but he took one look at the directions and said, "I changed my mind. I won't have time for planes. I'll be too busy helping Jack with his car."

"I'm working on a P-38," Maxie said. "Same as Ari. You should see how nice his turned out. And it looks easy to do."

"Everything looks easy when somebody else does it," I said.

Mrs. Lasker let the kids work on their planes in class whenever they finished their work. Shepsy was building a P-47 solid. He was doing such a great job on it, I figured my plane didn't have much of a chance. I even told him I was sure he'd win the contest.

"Are you entering?" he asked.

"I plan to. I built a P-38. It's all finished."

"Why don't you bring it to school tomorrow. I'd like to see it."

"I'm afraid to walk around with it too much. It might fall apart. Why don't you come over to my house after school today, and I'll show it to you."

"I can't after school. I have to practice piano. How about after Hebrew?"

"Sure," I said.

At Hebrew that afternoon, before we began our Jewish history, Mr. Kolodny started talking to us about Hitler and Germany and how the Jews of Europe were being burned and gassed in concentration camps.

"So much of our history is being repeated right now —today—in our own time," he said, removing his *yarmulke* to smooth down his hair. "It is a repeat of what has gone on before, in past generations, in past centuries, in other countries, under other Hitlers."

The room grew silent as he spoke of the madness in Europe. You can expect to read about madness in history books, but it's frightening to realize that it can still be going on.

Then the kids began to talk. Almost everyone told about aunts, uncles, cousins and grandparents who were no longer heard from, who had mysteriously disappeared—just like my Aunt Etta and her family.

Even when Hebrew was over, I couldn't get the conversation out of my mind. As Shepsy and I were walking up the stairs to my apartment, I said, "Do you realize that what's happening to the Jews in Europe could've been happening to *us* right now? We could have just as easily been born there—instead of here."

"That's right," said Shepsy. "It was just a matter of geography . . . and luck." He wiped his hair off his forehead. "You know something? It kind of gives me the jitters to think that you and I . . . we could be . . . dead." And we both got so scared, we ran all the way up the stairs.

I introduced Shepsy to my mother as *Shepsy from Hebrew School*, and her whole face lit up. She couldn't do enough for him. She even took off his jacket and hung it up in the closet.

"You don't have to do that, Mrs. Stein," he said. "I just came up for a second to look at Ari's plane."

My mother reached into her apron pocket and took something out. "Why don't you call your mother and ask her if you can stay for supper?" she said, handing him a nickel. "We're having veal."

"That's a great idea," I said. "Will you stay?"

"Yeah, if I can. Thanks."

We went down to the ground floor, where the phone was, and Shepsy called home for permission to eat over. "We're having veal," he said. Then he hung up.

Before supper I took him to my room and showed him my P-38. "It's a beauty," he said. "All the time I've been thinking that I had a pretty good chance of winning that contest. But now I'm not so sure."

I had to laugh. "That's funny. When I saw *your* plane, I decided that I was the one who didn't have a chance."

"Maybe both of us will win," he said. He punched me in the arm.

"Maybe neither of us will win," I said. I punched him back.

Shepsy ran his finger over the top of the plane. "You know something? I wish our planes were real and we could fly them over Germany and get those Nazis."

"Do you think it's as bad over there as everyone says it is?"

"Sure. Maybe even worse. My dad says thousands of Jews are being murdered in those concentration camps every day."

I thought about what Shepsy said. Thousands every day. At that rate the thousands would grow into millions. And I wondered about my aunt and my uncle and my cousins. Were they part of those millions? Had they already waited their turns at the gas chambers?

Mr. Kolodny told us later that the Jews marched to the gas chambers with a prayer on their lips. The prayer, *Ani Maamin—I believe.*

I saw a lot more of Shepsy after that day at my house, especially on Saturdays. It all began one Saturday in early October, when he came over during lunch and invited me to join a club.

"It's a Sabbath club," he said. "A few guys get together at a *shtiebel* over on Neptune Avenue. We eat and sing and discuss things and eat some more and just sort of spend an afternoon together. I thought you might like to come along."

When my mother heard *Sabbath club* and *shtiebel*, she began humming and offered Shepsy a plate of chopped liver.

"No thanks, Mrs. Stein. We do a lot of eating at the club."

My mother beamed when I told Shepsy I would walk with him to the *shtiebel* to see what was doing.

A *shtiebel* is a synagogue. But it's not like an ordinary synagogue because it's usually very small and it's often not even in a building of its own. A *shtiebel* was once a store or an apartment or a little house that a rabbi and a group of people took over. And it's not organized like a synagogue. There's no president, no board of directors and no women's organization. Just a rabbi and people. People who come to pray and to learn the Torah and Talmud. There are a lot of these synagogues all over Brooklyn. This one is in a small, two-story, white frame house. Shepsy pointed it out at Neptune Avenue and Ocean Parkway.

"The *shtiebel* is downstairs," he said. "It's been

around as long as I can remember. My dad says it's been around as long as he can remember too."

We went up the walk to the door, and Shepsy opened it. I felt funny walking into a strange house without knocking first. We stood in the hallway, and off to the side I could see a large room which once was the living room and where men were now learning Jewish law.

"The rabbi lives in the upstairs apartment," Shepsy whispered. "You'll see him later. He's an old man with a long, white beard. My dad says he was always an old man with a long, white beard."

"Is the rabbi the one who runs the club?" I asked.

"No," said Shepsy. "The guy who leads us is a high school yeshiva boy, Izzy Novitsky."

We walked across the hall to a small room. Inside, a group of about six kids my age was sitting on chairs in a semicircle, listening to an older kid, who was sitting on a table in front of them.

Izzy Novitsky was talking about the Jewish return to Palestine. "If we had Palestine today, the European Jews could have been saved," he was saying. "It's too late for them—they're doomed. But we need Palestine for the future. For a Jewish homeland. So that Jews will always have a place to go, so nothing like this can ever happen to them again."

When Izzy finished talking, the kids took a break, and Shepsy introduced me. Izzy welcomed me to the club and asked what kinds of things I wanted to do there.

"Sing," I told him.

"Good," he said. "Because we do a lot of that here." And we did too. We sang Hebrew songs and Sabbath songs. We ate cake and drank soda. We held discussions and interpreted passages from the Bible. But mostly we sang. And I loved the singing most of all—and the *Havdalah*.

Havdalah is the ceremony that ushers out the Sabbath. After sunset we walked across the hall to the large room where the men were. The room was in darkness except for the light from a double-wick candle resting on a small table, and I could just make out the rabbi in his *kapaute*, his long, black gabardine coat. In one hand he held a cup of wine and in the other hand, a box of spices.

Izzy went over and picked up the candle and held it while the rabbi said the blessing over the wine and the blessing over the spices. He passed the spice box around for all of us to smell. Spices—to lift the spirit, to refresh the soul. Then he said the blessing over the light of the candle, and we all spread our hands toward the candlelight to feel the heat of the flame and to see the light on our fingertips. We bring the Sabbath in with light. We usher it out with light. Finally, the rabbi and some of the men took turns sipping the wine, and we all gathered together for the singing of *"Hamavdil,"* the song which signifies the separation of the holy from the everyday, and *"Eliyahu Ha-Navi,"* a song about Elijah, the prophet, a song made even more beautiful by the darkness and stillness of the room.

And there in the darkness, with just the light from that double flame, we sang, all of us, grouped around the rabbi with the long, white beard and the long, black coat. And for me, the Sabbath became the Sabbath once again.

16

From that time on, I spent all my Saturdays with Shepsy. We'd go to services together every Saturday morning, sometimes at his synagogue, sometimes at mine and sometimes at the *shtiebel*. From there we'd go either to his house or mine for lunch, and then to the club.

The afternoons at the *shtiebel* became more and more enjoyable as I came to know the other kids better. Izzy began teaching us how to conduct services, and I was almost always the cantor.

Saturday became very special to me again. It was no longer just another ordinary day. I found that I spent most of the week with Maxie, but all my Saturdays were with Shepsy. I felt comfortable with him. Comfortable in a way I knew I could never be with Maxie—as much as I liked him.

One Saturday after Shepsy and I had lunch at my house and were starting out for the club, we saw Maxie and Brownie sitting on the curb in front of 2–4.

"Hey Ari," Maxie called. "You want to come down to the boardwalk with us?"

"Not today, Maxie. Thanks."

"Where have you been disappearing to on Saturdays lately?"

"Yeah," Brownie said. "Your old pals ain't good enough for you anymore?"

"Sure you are, Brownie," I said. "But I've joined a club that meets on Saturdays."

"You belong to a club and didn't even ask us to join?"

"I would have, but I didn't think you'd be interested."

"What kind of club is it?" Maxie asked.

"A Sabbath club," I said.

"You're right," Brownie said. "I ain't interested."

"Same here," said Maxie.

Then Buddy came running up Nass Walk, waving and shouting, "My big chance! My big chance!"

"What's up?" Maxie asked, as Buddy collapsed on the curb.

"It's finally come," he said between breaths. "The chance I've been waiting for. My big break."

"You mean you've been discovered?" I asked.

"Not yet. But I will be by Wednesday."

"What's doing Wednesday?" Maxie asked.

So Buddy went on to tell us how Wednesday night is Amateur Night at the Loew's Coney Island Theater. And when he gets up on that stage to do his Frank Sinatra impersonation, some secret talent scout who'll probably be sitting in the audience will discover him and take him to Hollywood.

134

"I wanted to do it last year," he said, "but I didn't take my acting career too seriously then."

"I thought you forgot all about being discovered," I said. "You haven't been uptown for a long time."

"That's because my ma won't let me go, now that vacation is over. She says that with school and homework I don't have time to waste running all the way uptown for nonsense. And I should concentrate on my education and make something of myself, so I won't turn into a bum."

"Hey Buddy," I said. "Are you sure your mother isn't Jewish?"

"I'm sure," he said, laughing. "I guess she's just a mother. Anyway, I'd better go home and start practicing. I'll see you guys later."

"What's all this about an amateur night?" I asked Maxie when Buddy was gone.

"Some of the theaters try to promote business on the weekdays. So they put on an amateur night once a week or so, and a bunch of kids come to sing or dance or something. At the end of the contest everybody claps, and the one who gets the most claps wins a prize."

"Can Buddy really sing?"

"Well, he's got a good reputation, but I don't know of anyone who's ever heard him."

"I still say he's dreamin'," Brownie said.

"Sometimes all we have are our dreams," I heard myself saying, and I laughed to myself.

135

"Huh?" Brownie said.

"Nothing," I said.

Between Saturday and Wednesday Buddy rounded up every kid in the neighborhood, and asked them to come to the theater to listen to him sing and to clap for him afterward. He promised each kid an autographed picture of himself after he became a famous movie star.

Wednesday night at seven, Maxie and I went downstairs to pick up Buddy. While we were waiting for him in the hallway, we heard his mother yelling at him in Italian. When he came out, Maxie asked, "What was that all about?"

"Oh, it's just my ma. She says I'd better not get discovered tonight. She doesn't want me running off to Hollywood."

Buddy sure was sharp-looking. He had on a pair of navy blue pants, a light blue sport jacket and a bow tie. "Do I look like Sinatra?" he asked.

"From the bow tie down," I said.

We met Brownie and Lippy outside, and we all headed for Loew's Coney Island Theater.

"Jack's comin' too," Brownie said. "He's a good clapper."

The theater was crowded and noisy. We wished Buddy good luck, and found seats next to Shepsy and some kids from our block.

The first contestant was a guy who sang "Chattanooga Choo Choo." He was pretty good. Then came a girl who sang something about leaving her heart at the stage-door canteen. She was even better. Then a couple of girls did a little tap dance, and they were just fair. Then on came our Buddy Rizzo, and a loud cheer went up from his fans.

Buddy got up on the stage, held the microphone out in front of him and in his best Sinatra style started to sing, "All of me, why not take all of me. . . ."

Boy, was he lousy! He was so off-tune, it was terrible. I slid down in my seat, I was so embarrassed. And the more he sang, the further down I slid. I don't know why I was embarrassed. I wasn't the one who was singing. I guess I was embarrassed for him. But he just kept at it. And the funny thing is, every time he sang, "Why not take all of me?" all these crazy girls in the audience started to moan, "Oh Buddy." They were falling out of their seats and looked like they were fainting or dying or something. And it was all for real. I know for a fact that Buddy didn't invite girls to come and clap for him. I guess they were so busy looking at his beautiful face that they couldn't hear his lousy voice.

There were about ten contestants. At the end of the contest they all stood in a line on the stage. The master of ceremonies walked over to each one and held his hand over the person's head. That meant it was time to clap. When he got to Buddy's head, his loyal fans cheered and clapped and the girls went wild too. It was an easy win. Buddy got ten free passes to the Loew's Coney Island Theater.

When it was all over, Buddy jumped off the stage and ran over to us. "Hey you guys. I won. How did you like my performance?"

"Well, you sure had those girls swooning," I told him.

"You sure gave it everything you had," Maxie said.

"You were lousy," Brownie said. "Let's go home."

"You go if you want to," Buddy told him. "I'm waiting around for a while. There might be a talent scout looking for me."

So we hung around and waited. A half hour maybe. "What's the use?" Buddy said. "We might as well go. Nobody's coming for me."

"Maybe the talent scout couldn't make it tonight," I told him.

"Yeah," said Maxie. "With the war on and everything, maybe there's a shortage of talent scouts. Maybe they're all in the army or looking for talent at the USO."

I put my hand on Frank Sinatra's shoulder. "Come on, Buddy. There's always next time."

"Sure," he said, trying hard to smile.

17

I can always tell it's November by the cold, gray sky. The days were getting shorter and colder, and just about the only thing that brightened them was the thought of the model-plane contest and Thanksgiving vacation.

On the Tuesday before Thanksgiving, Buddy, Lippy and I brought our planes to school and set them up in the gym to await the judging the next day. Maxie had never got around to building his plane.

When school was over that day and the five of us started for home, we heard the honk of a car, and a shiny, black '32 Ford pulled up alongside us. I couldn't believe my eyes. It was Jack. And his car was really working. It didn't sound so good, but boy, it was a terrific-looking machine, spotless and brilliant, and all four tires were on it. I never thought he'd get that thing moving.

"Anyone want to go for a spin around the block?" Jack shouted above the roar of the engine.

"You bet!" Brownie cried, as he and Lippy flung open the door and jumped into the front seat. Maxie opened the back door, and he and Buddy jumped in too.

"Aren't you coming?" Maxie asked me.

"I've got to be back by four," I said.

"We're just going around the block. Aren't we, Jack?"

"Sure," Jack said. "We'll be home in a couple of minutes. Hop in."

I stood there for a second, trying to decide what to do, when I saw five sets of eyes staring at me, waiting for an answer. Don't go, I told myself. Don't go. Tell them you're going home to eat and then straight to Hebrew. Tell them you'll go another time.

The five sets of eyes were still on me. "You coming or not?" Jack yelled. "I don't have all day."

"Okay," I said, getting into the backseat. "As long as we're just going around the block."

Jack pulled away from the curb with such speed that I almost fell out the door. The engine was making so much noise that I was sure Jack couldn't hear me when I said to Maxie, "Hey, I just remembered something. Jack's only sixteen. He doesn't have a license."

"So what if he doesn't have a license?" Maxie shouted. "He can drive, can't he?"

"A license is just a piece of paper, kid," Jack shouted over his shoulder. Then he laughed. "I don't have insurance either. Nothing matters as long as you know how to drive."

I hope you drive better than you play the trumpet, I wanted to say. But I didn't.

We took a few spins around the neighborhood, and then Jack said, "Let's see how this baby moves on Ocean Parkway."

We drove along Ocean Parkway for a while, and I kept waiting for Jack to turn back. But he didn't. He kept going and going, and the next thing I knew, we had gone all the way to Prospect Park. We circled the park a few times, and then Jack started back down Ocean Parkway toward home. "Okay, baby!" he shouted. "Let's see what you can do." And he tore down the parkway at about a hundred miles an hour, screeching and swerving, narrowly missing every car in our path. I lurched forward and almost fell off the seat. I grabbed hold of Maxie and closed my eyes. I felt the roaring and rumbling of the wheels. I heard all the guys laughing and shouting.

"Terrific, Jack!"

"Beautiful!"

"Let 'er go!"

"Faster, Jack, faster!"

They were nuts. The whole bunch of them. And me too, for being there. And then a terrifying thing happened. In the darkness I felt myself flying. Flying in my father's milk truck, across all the years of my life. Over Rivington Street and Luna Park and Nass Walk. Over all the synagogues I had ever been in, over all the roofs I had ever been on. And my mother and father and all the people I had ever known were on these roofs, crying.

"Such a short life."

"Pity, he would have become a great cantor."

"Poor Lionel. He was right about The Melting Pot."

The sudden blasting of a thousand car horns made me jump right out of my dream. Jack was tearing down the parkway toward an intersection. The light was green, but as we sped toward it, it flashed to red. He didn't even slow down.

I screamed. "Are you crazy? Stop for the light!"

He slammed on the brakes, and we skidded into the intersection—into the path of an oncoming car. Maxie grabbed hold of me. I could feel him trembling and my own heart pounding. The other car came screeching toward us. Not a second too soon it swerved and skidded to a halt.

The car leaped across the intersection, and Jack must've panicked or something because he burst into another fury of speed. He went wild, weaving in and out of traffic all the way down Ocean Parkway. But this time there was no laughing, no shouting. Only pale faces, open mouths and arms clutching each other.

The car skidded off the parkway, whipped along the side streets, jumped a curb and plowed into some wooden crates in front of Hymie's Grocery. I fell forward, hitting my head against the front seat. Jack backed the car off the curb just as Hymie came running out of his store. We left him waving violently as we drove away and plowed through the streets until we came to a sudden halt in front of 2–4 Nass Walk.

The same God that delivered the Children of Israel

out of the land of Egypt delivered the Nass Walk boys out of Jack Brown's car.

I jumped out and yelled, "You know what, Jack? You're a maniac. And you're a lousy trumpet player too."

I didn't know where Jack and the others were going, and I didn't care. All I know is, I ran all the way up to the roof and crouched on the floor behind Mrs. Silverman's sheets, shaking and shivering all over. Then Maxie ran up after me, and we huddled and shivered together. And for a long time neither of us spoke.

I sat there, trembling and wishing that everything that had happened was just a dream. That I'd wake up pretty soon and everything would be right and normal again. And then I remembered Maxie's words— "Heck, Ari. This *is* normal."

Well, normal for them maybe, but not normal for me. Maybe it was their way, but it wasn't mine.

And I remembered some other words too—"If I am not for myself, who will be for me?"

After a while Maxie said, "Boy, Ari. Were we ever lucky!"

"It was more than luck," I said. "It was a miracle that saved us. Do you realize we were almost killed?" Then I started shivering all over again, just thinking of God's miracle.

"I guess we'll have to get used to danger if we're going to be FBI men," he said.

"You know what, Maxie? I don't give two hoots about becoming an FBI man or becoming an All-American Boy either. I'll settle for being a *mockey*. If I were a *mockey*, I'd be in Hebrew right now instead of hiding on the roof with this bump on my head."

And then more words: *I believe, Ani Maamin.* Jews had faith even in the face of death. All I was facing was Maxie Friedman. Where was my faith? Hebrew School! There was still time. I got up and took my *yarmulke* out of my pocket. Then I put it back where it belonged—on my head.

18

The next morning we sneaked through the alleys so we wouldn't have to pass Hymie's Grocery. Brownie and Lippy wore sunglasses so they wouldn't be recognized. And boy, did they look dumb! There wasn't a ray of sun in that whole cold, gray sky.

"What happened to you guys after the crash?" Maxie asked.

"I ran straight home," Buddy said.

"That's what I did," said Lippy.

"Me and Jack—we ran home and jumped into bed and hid under the covers," Brownie said.

"What happened to the car?" I asked.

"It's sittin' in the alley. The whole front's bashed in. Jack's mad as hell. My old man's makin' him sell it for junk."

"Your father is exercising very wise judgment," I said.

"What's that mean?"

"Forget it."

Toward the end of the day, an eighth-grade kid walked into our room to announce the winners of the contest. First he announced the first- and second-place winners of the flying models. I didn't recognize any of the names. But I recognized the name of the first-place winner of the solid models, all right. Ari Stein!

Shepsy gave me a couple of pats on the shoulder, and the rest of the class gave out a lot of yippees and hurrays and held up their fingers in a V for victory.

I won a Spitfire flying model. When put together, it would be gigantic—three feet long. Boy, not a bad prize for a *mockey*!

"It sure is a beauty," Maxie said on the way home.

"Sure is. This is the kind of plane the British used to beat the pants off the Germans in the Battle of Britain. I wish I could get to work on it right now."

"Why don't you?" Maxie asked. "We'll help. Won't we, guys?"

"Sure," Brownie said.

"No thanks, fellas. I'd like to show it to my mother, and then I've got to get to Hebrew."

"Aw, come on, Ari. You and your Hebrew. Why don't you stick around and we'll celebrate your victory."

"No, Maxie. I'm going to Hebrew. We'll celebrate tomorrow. It's Thanksgiving." I felt the bump on my head. I sure did have a lot to be thankful for.

The gray days of November were gone, and December came, cold and clear and without snow. For two whole weeks before Chanukah, my mother kept talking about calling off her trip to Chicago.

"Maybe I shouldn't go, Abe."

"Nonsense, Sarah. Go and enjoy yourself."

"But I've never been away from you and Ari before."

"Then it's time you had a little vacation."

"But on Chanukah . . . I should be with my family."

"Leah is your family too."

"But a week is such a long time. I'll worry about you."

"We'll get along just fine. Won't we, Ari?"

"Sure, Ma. You don't have to worry. I'll be with Maxie."

"That's what worries me. Ari, do you have to spend so much time with him?"

"Maxie's a good guy, Ma."

"But he doesn't go to *shul*. He doesn't go to Hebrew School. What will become of him? What will become of you?"

"I don't think we have to worry about Ari," my father said, and he put a hand on my shoulder and smiled.

"Sure, Ma. I'll be okay. And Maxie . . . he'll be okay too . . . in his own way."

My mother was leaving on a Sunday morning. And as I sat on her bed and watched her pack, I knew that there was something I had to tell her. I would never feel right about myself if I didn't. So right then and there I told her how I took the money from the tea can and how I was going to buy her all those hats and coats and send her to Chicago. And the only thing I ended up buying her was a feather.

When I looked at my mother, I expected to see the faraway look on her face. But instead there was a smile. She gave me a quick hug and a kiss and didn't say a word.

I heard the honk of a horn and ran to the window. "She's here!" I shouted.

"We're all ready," my father said, picking up the suitcase.

We made our way down the stairs, and when we got to the ground floor, my mother stopped at the mailbox. "If a letter comes . . . if you hear from . . ."

"Yes, Sarah. If we get a letter from Etta, we'll let you know."

Maxie was outside, giving the '41 Mercury the once-over. He was holding some crazy contraption that resembled a shovel covered with a piece of window screen.

"Hey, Maxie. Whatcha got there?"

He held it close for me to see. "A shovel that I covered up with a piece of window screen."

"Yeah, that's what I thought. Say, Maxie, you want to come to the station with us?"

"No thanks. In fact, I was just going to ask you if you want to come with me. I'm taking this thing and going off to strain the beach."

"Strain the beach?"

"Yeah. I don't know why I didn't think of it before. At the end of summer there's a ton of lost coins hidden in the sand—and jewelry too. Guys have been straining for months now. But there's plenty of beach left for you and me. There's a million dollars out there. Come on, Ari. Forget the train and come along. We'll make a fortune."

"A fortune? It seems to me that I've heard that story before. So no thanks, Maxie. I'm going to the station."

I started to walk away but turned back to ask a question that had long been on my mind. "Say, Maxie. About the boardwalk . . . exactly how much can you see under there?"

"Can you keep a secret, Ari?"

"Sure I can."

"I can't see a thing."

"Thanks, Maxie. And you know something? I can't either."

My father put the suitcase in the car, and the three of us piled in. "Hi, Aunt Malkeh," I said for the fun of it. She gave me a funny kind of look and drove off.

A light snow started to fall. Maybe Maxie and I could go sledding at Prospect Park. I turned around to look at him. He was standing near the street sign where I first met him that June Monday, holding the strainer with one hand and waving to me with the other.